ME

and my

BIG MOUTH

The Second Book of Tanith

Jenny Sullivan

PONT

To my Best Boys:
Rob, Bill, Darren, Ian, Conall,
David and Mike
with love.

First Impression—2002

ISBN 1 84323 067 4

Printed in Wales at
Gomer Press, Llandysul, Ceredigion

MAIN CHARACTERS

Tanith Williams	Now nearly seventeen
Gwydion	Formerly a white cat – but also a Shapeshifter. Now Dragonking of Ynys Haf
Teleri Angharad Probert	Tanith's best friend – known as T.A.
Mam	Tanith's mother
The Ant	Chief Daughter of the Moon – Tanith's Aunt Antonia (and five other Aunts, who, together with Tanith, form the Circle of Seven)
Mr Howard	Once Tanith's School Music Teacher, who is also Taliesin, Bard and Friend to Great Merlin – but only in Ynys Haf
Heledd	Tanith's older sister
Cariad	Heledd's daughter
Aunty Fliss	Tanith's Aunt Felicity, now living in Ynys Haf to escape the effects of Alzheimer's Disease, a terrible illness which only affects her in the Real Time world
Iestyn	Her husband and leader of the Ynys Haf community
Nest	Gwydion's Half-Tylwyth Teg Aunt who lives in Ynys Haf
O'Liam of the Green Boots	A Leprechaun
Gwyddno Garanhir	Lord of the Sixteen Doomed Cities of Cantre'r Gwaelod
Elffin	His son (for whom T.A. has rather a Soft Spot)

– AND NOT FORGETTING THE BADDIES –

Merch Corryn Du	Spiderwitch – Astarte Perkins's (see *The Magic Apostrophe*) Great-Great-Ever-so-many-Greats-Grandmother, the Wickedest Witch of All . . .
Conor of the Land Beneath	The sinister Leprechaun King
Maebh	A beautiful but rather dim Irish Princess, great-great-great grand-daughter of the Spiderwitch
Master Henbane	Maebh's 'minder' – who is using her to gain control of Ynys Haf
Rhiryd ap Rhiryd Goch	Evil Sons of the Evil Lord Rhiryd Goch, who wanted to be High King of Ynys Haf

and his twin brothers
Ardwyn and Jason

AND OTHER CHARACTERS YOU HAVE STILL TO MEET IN

Me and My Big Mouth!

1

At first, I tried to ignore it. The note, I mean, the one from Conor of the Land Beneath. But after a while it began to feel a bit like trying to ignore a really bad toothache. T.A. didn't help, either. Every time I saw her, she asked, 'So, what are you going to do about it?' until I wanted to smack her, very hard, even if she is my best mate.

I hadn't mentioned it to Mam or the Aunts – since I'm the Lady of Ynys Haf, it's up to me to decide what to do, right? The trouble was, I was beginning to feel guilty that I wasn't actually doing anything about it at all. It was beginning to colour my outlook on life, and when that happens I get generally bad-tempered and ratty. In the end, I fetched the note out of the drawer and took it downstairs to show to Mam. That's what Mams are for, right? To listen and get you out of trouble when you need to be rescued. Not that I was in trouble right at that moment – but it probably wouldn't be long before I was.

She was peeling potatoes at the sink, and singing. She was off in a little world of her own, and I had to shout to make her hear me over the chorus of an ancient Beatles song and the running tap.

'Mam!' I bellowed, and, startled, she turned round.

'Good grief, Tansy, what on earth's the matter?' she asked, dropping the potato peeler into the sink.

'I've sort of got a problem,' I said, and put the note on the kitchen table. She dried her hands on a tea-towel and picked it up. I didn't have to read over her shoulder: I knew it off by heart. It was written on a tiny piece of paper in crabby brown script.

'To the Lady Tan'ith of Ynys Haf:'

it said,

'You stole O'Liam Ironfinder from me, and you gave me a promise.

By all the Laws of all the Kingdoms of All the World, you have a Promise to keep and amends to make.'

Then, underneath,

'Forgetting a debt does not pay it.'

It was signed with a big, wobbly cross, and the words 'The Mark of Conor, Lord of the Land Beneath'. Conor can't read or write – he keeps lots of ancient scribes to do that for him. But that's about the only thing Conor can't do. Conor is the very scary Lord of the Leprechauns, and I may be the Lady of Ynys Haf, but he scares me stiff.

Mam finished reading the note and looked up, frowning. 'Why on earth didn't you show this to me earlier, Tanith? This isn't something you can ignore and hope it goes away!'

'I know,' I said, miserably. 'Only I didn't know what to do with it, Mam.' I'd told her all about the adventures – and the problems – I'd had with O'Liam Ironfinder, a genius of a leprechaun, and Maebh (both of them also from the Land Beneath) while she and Dad were on holiday, but I hadn't told her about the note. Didn't want to worry her, I suppose. Also, I think a little bit of me hoped it might go away if I didn't think about it!

'I know you rescued O'Liam Ironfinder and his green boots, and in Conor's eyes I suppose that counts as stealing what he considers rightly his, but what on earth does the bit about a promise mean?'

'Well, when we – Nest and I – were trying to get Conor to help us to find Gwydion, he wouldn't unless we promised him something. I thought I was being really crafty, not offering him anything, making him pick what he wanted, so that I could be sure I could give it him without putting anyone in danger.'

'And?'

'Well, what he wanted was Maebh. Still immortal, but without her magic. So I said I'd give her to him. And then, in all the fuss and bother – over getting Gwydion back and up-to-date with what he'd missed and all that – I, well, I sort of forgot, and let her go,' I muttered lamely. 'I didn't like the idea of handing her over to him, anyway, even if she was a baddie. It doesn't seem right, somehow.'

Mam was staring at me. 'You mean Nest let you make a promise to a leprechaun – and Conor of the Land Beneath into the bargain?' she said.

I nodded, miserably. 'It wasn't Nest's fault, Mam,' I said, 'I'm the Lady – I made the promise.'

Mam sat down at the kitchen table, the note still held in her hand. 'Well, what are you going to do about it?' she asked.

'Me?' I said, stupidly.

'Oh, for goodness sake, Tanz,' Mam said exasperatedly. 'Who else? Honestly, it's time you took responsibility for the decisions you make. And while I'm at it, you need some new knickers – and your bedroom's a pig-sty.'

'Pardon?' I blinked at the confusing change of subject, and then realised why when I heard someone open the back door. It was Heledd, laden with shopping bags, with her little daughter Caroline-Adelaide (but everyone calls her Cariad) shrieking and kicking, almost upside-down under her arm. Cariad's face was bright red, and I jumped up and rescued her, turned her the right way up and blew a raspberry on her nose.

'Hello, lovely,' Mam gave Heledd a kiss and a hug. I didn't. I get on loads better with her than I used to when she lived at home, but if I kissed her she'd think I'd finally flipped.

'Hiya, Tanz,' Hel said, dumping her shopping on the floor and sinking into one of the kitchen chairs. 'Put the kettle on and make me a cup of tea, there's a dear. I'm absolutely exhausted.'

I thought about asking what her last servant had died of, but decided it wasn't worth the hassle. I dumped Cariad onto the floor and filled the kettle. My niece is walking, now, and is a little sweetheart – sometimes. She has a temper like a fire-cracker when she's crossed. Mam and I really hope she grows out of it, quick, because according to Merlin, she will have rather a lot of magical powers when she's thirteen, just as I did. And if she's still having tantrums then, it could be a bit hairy – or froggy – for anyone who gets in her way…

I made the tea and poured everyone a cup,

including my niece, who has hers very milky in a special, unspillable plastic cup – well, that's what the manufacturers thought, anyway. They didn't know Cari!

Hel took a slurp and then dived into her carrier bags. 'Look,' she said, as if we hadn't noticed, 'I've been shopping!' She pulled out dresses and skirts and shorts and tops and shoes and sandals and a very small bikini.

Mam raised her eyebrows. 'You've been spending, Heledd! Does Siôn know?'

'Of course. It was his idea. He's won a competition at work for best performance by an under-sales-manager. We're going to Bermuda for two whole weeks!'

'Wow!' I said, 'you lucky dab!'

'And Siôn said, seeing as we didn't have to pay for the holiday, I ought to go and get myself a few new things.'

Mam eyed the vast pile. 'A few! I hope Siôn got a good bonus this year, because this lot must have cost as much as the holiday would have.'

'Don't be daft, Mam. Anyway, what I wondered was, could you and Dad have Cari for us while we're away? Tanz will be home to help you, now she's on holiday from school, so the baby won't be any real trouble, will she? Oh, please, Mam? It's the chance of a lifetime, a holiday in Bermuda.'

I took a slurp of my tea to hide my grin. I knew perfectly well that Mam would love to have Cari – but she wasn't going to let on to Hel. Sure enough, Mam frowned.

'Well, I don't know, love,' she said, as if she really meant it. 'Your Dad and I, well, we aren't getting any younger, and the baby's quite a handful.'

Cariad, perfectly aware that she was being discussed, gazed up at her Mam-gu and gave her a big grin. Mam melted.

'Oh, all right then. When are you off?'

'That's the thing, Mam. The day after tomorrow. It's the only time Siôn could take leave, so we fly out from Gatwick on Sunday morning, early. So if you could have her tomorrow night…'

Mam sighed. 'Oh, all right. But for goodness sake remember to pack her purple cat this time. Last time she shrieked half the night, and we couldn't get into your place to get it for her.'

'I'll give you a key, just in case,' Hel said, shoving clothes back into carrier bags.

So that was that, then. We were going to have Cariad for a fortnight. Hel finished her tea, and I carried the baby out to the car and strapped her into her baby-seat. While I was bending over, she grabbed my nose and made my eyes water.

'Doppit!' I said, and Cariad fell about laughing.

When Hel had driven off, I went back into the kitchen.

'Which is going to be another problem,' Mam said, piling the cups and saucers into the sink.

'What?'

'Well, I can't come to Ynys Haf with you if I've got the baby to look after, can I?'

'I'm going to Ynys Haf?' I said, stupidly. 'Why?'

'Because,' Mam said grimly, 'you owe Conor a

girlfriend and a leprechaun. And one thing you do not do, my girl, is break a promise to Conor of the Land Beneath.'

I think I knew all along that that was what she'd say. But she hadn't finished, yet.

She swished the cups in sudsy water. 'Have a chat with Aunt Ant before you go,' she said, 'see if she's got any good ideas. Pity all the other Aunts aren't here, but the Daughters of the Moon seem to have become horribly scattered recently. One or other of them is always gallivanting off somewhere. I suppose now you're the Lady, they've all sort of retired and let you take over. But at least Ant is home at the moment.'

We went round to see the Ant later that evening, after tea. The Ant's real name is Antonia, and she is the sort of Senior Witch in the family. We call her The Ant because she's tall, and dark, and thin, and always busy. She lives in this huge, rambling house which has some seriously weird dimensions – i.e., they aren't there at all unless you know where to look! She opened the door wearing a long purple robe thing, with her glasses dangling round her neck on a chain. She was carrying a book. It wasn't a spell-book, or some ancient volume full of folk-lore. It had a neon pink cover and was called *True Love and Tina Thomas.*

'Still reading rubbish I see, Ant,' Mam said teasingly.

Ant scowled. 'This isn't rubbish, Gen,' she protested. 'It's research. I'm always intrigued to see the way mortals get themselves into such a pickle over a little thing like love. Honestly, it's research.'

Yeah, in a pig's ear! Aunt Ant loved trashy romances, but would never admit it in a million years. She put the book aside, and we went into the kitchen, which was where important family conferences always seemed to take place, whoever's house we were in! Mam explained my problem.

'Oh, dear me, Tansy,' Ant sighed. 'You do get yourself into some first-class messes, *ferch*, don't you? Of all the people to tangle with, Conor of the Land Beneath is one of the worst.'

'I blame Merlin,' Mam put in. 'If it hadn't been for his stupid meddling in the affairs of Ynys Haf – "testing" Tanith, he said he was, to see if she was worthy to be Gwydion's Dragonqueen. The cheek of that man! Of course she's going to be Dragonqueen. It's in the legend. I'd give him a piece of my mind, if I knew where he was.'

She would, too. My Mam isn't scared of anyone.

We discussed the whys and wherefores for a while, but at the end, Aunt Ant agreed with Mam: I had to go back to Ynys Haf, and sort things out, quick. Still, at least Gwydion would be there to help me this time – last time he'd slept through the whole thing!

2

I could have gone whizzing off to Ynys Haf from Aunt Ant's house, I suppose, but I had to see T.A. before I left. She'd never forgive me if I went without telling her. She probably wouldn't forgive me for going without her, either, but Mam and Aunt Ant thought it was better she stayed behind.

She was dead ratty. 'Call yourself a friend?' she said furiously. 'You're going off to Ynys Haf and leaving me behind? I can't believe you'd do that, Tanz!'

'Mam thinks it'll be too dangerous for you to come,' I said, miserably. 'Honest, T.A., I'd much rather you came with me, but since Conor of the Land Beneath went and put a spell on you last time, it probably isn't a good idea for you to be anywhere near him.'

T.A. looked scornful. 'You surely don't think I'd let that little creep get at me a second time, do you? I should have known better than to trust him last time, him and his silken threads and stuff.'

'Yes, well,' I said.

'Yes, well what? What do you mean by that?'

'Nothing. I want you with me, honestly I do. But I don't want to put you into any danger.'

'And what about you? Who'll be looking out for you when you go and get yourself in trouble, that's what I'd like to know!'

'Gwydion,' I said. And then, 'but I don't need anyone to look out for me. I can look out for myself. I'm the Lady of Ynys Haf.'

'And don't you manage to get yourself into some fine messes, too, Lady or not!' she retorted.

'Oh, look, T.A., please don't quarrel with me. I've got to go tomorrow and you aren't making it any easier. I don't want to part bad friends with you.'

She scowled. 'I don't either. Oh, look, Tanz, I know you've got to go. It's just that I'll worry the whole time you're away. And I'll be bored stiff.'

'Don't worry. I'll be fine.' I wished I believed it myself.

'Well, don't forget to take some tea-bags and stuff for Aunty Fliss,' she said.

So, next day, when Mam drove me up to Brechfa and the Door in Time, I had a back-pack full of goodies. As soon as I'd gone, Mam was going to Heledd's to collect Cariad, so she wouldn't have much time to worry about me, but I knew she would anyway. She had that pre-occupied look.

We parked in the Forestry Commission car-park and walked up the hill to the bare top. The standing stones waited, and after a quick hug I settled the back-pack firmly on my back, muttered the right words in Old Welsh, and stepped between the grey monoliths. I was instantly back in Ynys Haf. I'd packed a waterproof and a warm sweater, because whenever I crossed I never knew what the weather would be like. The seasons there bear no relation to what the seasons are in My Time Wales.

A sweater was the last thing I needed: it was so hot that as soon as I stepped through I could feel little beads of perspiration breaking out on my nose. I was glad to be back, because I love Ynys Haf – but I couldn't help wishing it was for a better reason than sorting out my problem with Conor of the Land Beneath.

I looked around me. It looked as if the dry, hot weather had been around for a long while – the grass was dry and parched, and had died altogether in places. Great cracks zig-zagged across the bare, dusty soil, and it looked more like Death Valley than Ynys Haf!

I shouldered my back-pack and set off towards the *tŷ hir*. It was hot, sweaty work, walking, and when I reached the woods behind the village I was grateful for the shade of the trees. I altered my course to stop for a rest beside the little stream that ran through the wood, but when I reached it the stream-bed had barely a smear of water on the bottom. I began to worry, then. This wasn't Ynys Haf conditions, not at all. Ynys Haf was always green and pleasant: admittedly, when I'd first come through the Door in Time there had been deep snow – but that was when magic had interrupted the smooth running of the seasons. Ynys Haf never, ever suffered from extremes of temperature – and this was extreme. So, what was causing it?

The path stretched ahead of me, and all around the heat-haze shimmered, insects buzzed and birds perched on branches, apparently too hot and exhausted to sing. I knew how they felt. My back-pack was getting heavier by the minute, and by the time I reached the long-house I was about ready to drop, and so thirsty I could have drunk the entire stock of mineral water in my local Tesco back in my Time.

I tottered up to the door of the *tŷ hir* and lifted the latch. It was cooler, and dark inside, but when I went in, the house was empty. I wasn't surprised that there wasn't a fire because it was so hot, but I was fairly gobsmacked at the state of the place. It was filthy: dust lay on every surface, and there was a spiderweb stretching from the iron firedog where the cooking cauldron always hung right up to the sleeping platform at the far end of the hut. No one had been here for a while, that was obvious. But where was everyone? Surely Aunty Fliss and her husband Iestyn, and Nest, who lived with them hadn't just abandoned the place? That didn't make sense at all.

I unhitched my back-pack with a sigh of relief, and left it on the table. I opened the far door of the long-house (it has two doors opposite each other so that the cows and humans can go in and out easily: cows to the left, humans to the right!). I wandered outside to the well and lowered the bucket down the dark hole. I heard it splash when it reached the bottom, but when I hauled it up the bucket was filled with greenish, smelly liquid that might have been drinkable water once but certainly wasn't any more. Over beneath the yellowing trees stood the row of wood and wicker bee-hives. I went over to them, but there was no comforting buzz from inside. I bent down and tried to see inside, but they seemed to be empty and disused.

Now I was seriously worried. This was like a ghost town in an old Western. I was almost expecting a big ball of tumbleweed to go blowing past – except that there wasn't any wind to blow anything, anywhere. There was just heat, and a blazing sun beating down.

I went back inside and sat at the table chewing my little finger-nail – the one I keep just for chewing when I'm worried, OK? I was beginning to fill up with dread. Where was everyone? There was only one thing for it. I should have to go and look.

I left my back-pack in the long-house and went outside again, took a deep breath and concentrated hard on shape-shifting. I shrank down, and stretched my arms out. I grew a forked tail, strong curved wings with pale patches on them, and reddish feathers barred with black sprouted all over my body. I spread my wings, getting the feel of them, and gripped the dusty earth with my strong talons. Then I launched myself up into the hot, dry air, climbing up above dry trees and dying grass. There should have been a broad silver river threading its way to the sea, but all that was left was a thin, unenthusiastic trickle. Nevertheless I swooped down and took a drink while I could: I certainly needed it.

Then I took to the skies again, climbing up into the cloudless blue, heading for Castell Du. Gwydion should be there, with any luck. He could tell me what was going on.

But Castell Du, perched on its great black bastion of rock over the incoming tide – and even that seemed thick and sluggish, as if it were too hot and tired to bother – was as empty as the long-house had been. I swooped in through an arrow-slit, winging down dark passages, circling great empty halls and bedchambers, skimming the battlements and slipping silently into the chapel. The castle was as empty as a sea-shell.

Outside once more, I swooped down to the seashore and joined some apathetic seagulls at the water's edge, walking around in the cool water. I glanced into the deep caves that fringed the beach, flicked some water over my wings to cool me, and then took off again. To the village this time: there would surely be someone there.

But there wasn't. There, too, were empty cottages and huts; no smoke issued from any of the roof-holes, and even the blacksmith's fire was out and his smithy empty.

Now I was beginning to get frightened. My arms were beginning to ache from flying. There was only one other place to look. Castell y Ddraig. If there was no one there, I didn't know what I would do. I'd probably have to go back and ask Mam and Aunt Ant. They might have some ideas . . .

There was something bothering and niggling at me about my brief stop at the beach, but I couldn't work out what it was. It sort of perched at the back of my brain sending out little flashes, like the blue light on top of a police car. But what had been wrong? I decided to think about it later. First of all, I needed to find Gwydion.

I pointed my beak north, and set off. It was a long way, and my wings were aching unbearably by the time the mighty grey battlements appeared in the distance. Castell y Ddraig was perched on top of the great craggy outcrop that looked out over what would, one day, be called the Menai Straits.

Dreading what I'd find, I approached the castle from the front, swooping in across the drawbridge. There was no dragon guarding it, not any more. Once its task was finished it had stretched its crimson wings and headed for its eyrie in the high mountains. But there was sound, and my heart leapt joyfully. People, at last!

I swooped into the courtyard, perched on an open-topped cart with one broken wheel, and looked around for a familiar face. But there wasn't one. *I didn't know one single person in the courtyard!*

Suddenly something whizzed past me, and an arrow embedded itself into the wood of the cart. With a startled squawk I shot into the air and hurtled up to the battlements out of harm's way. Below in the cobbled courtyard a scrawny figure was taking aim, and a second arrow was launched at me, but missed. While he was notching a third to the longbow, I swooped down to get a look at him, then hopped over the wall to safety, quickly. It was a face I knew, unfortunately. There was another one exactly like it, somewhere. It was either Ardwyn ap Rhiryd Goch, or his brother, Jason. I thought I'd got rid of them the last time I'd been here, but here they were – well, one of them, at least – like a bad penny, turning up again. And if one brother was here, the other one – and their elder brother, Rhiryd ap Rhiryd – would almost certainly be around somewhere.

I couldn't see Gwydion happily living side-by-side with that trio, therefore it looked as though the baddies had captured the castle. So, where was Gwydion, and Aunty Fliss and Nest, and all the villagers? It was beginning to look bad.

I flew slowly round the castle, keeping below the battlements out of arrow range. I didn't have a clue where else to look. I could go to Cantre'r Gwaelod, ask Gwyddno Garanhir if he knew what was going on, but I was so tired that I should have to rest before I went anywhere else. The sun was going down, sinking redly over the island of Anglesey, and I would have to find a safe place for the night.

And then I heard something strange – and familiar, at the same time – coming out of an arrowslit in the landward wall of Castell y Ddraig. It sounded like someone talking to himself – in a very Irish accent.

'Ah, to be sure,' the voice said mournfully, 'it's a long day that has no yearning, and they say a man of courage never lost it, but courage has never been my strong point. And don't they say, also as well, that it's better to fight and run away than have to fight another day? But there's no place for me to run, not any more, there is not, so. And I can do without fighting entirely.'

There was only one person capable of mangling proverbs like that. I flew into the arrowslit, perched, and peered inside. It was very dark, but when my eyes got used to the darkness I could see that it was a small room, with dirty straw on the floor. A thick rope was attached to the wall, and at the other end of the rope was a familiar foot wearing a familiar green boot.

I flew into the room – cell, really, and perched on the floor. The leprechaun slumped miserably against the wall, his eyes shut.

'Sure, and the one bright spot in the darkness is that it's cool, I suppose,' he said, 'it being so hot outside. But that's small comfort for ending my days in such a way, it is.'

I shifted, shimmering into my own shape. 'You won't end your days at all, O'Liam of the Green Boots. Not if I've got anything to do with it, anyway.'

His eyes shot open. 'Ah, mercy! And is it yourself

I'm looking at or someone else entirely?' he said, perking up immediately. 'Is it you, Lady Tan'ith?'

'It is,' I said. 'And I think the very first thing we need to do is get you out of here, O'Liam dear!'

I shifted him into a mouse, shifted back into my red kite shape, and airlifted him out of there, leaving the padlocked, leather ankle cuff empty on the floor of the cell. That would give his captors something to scratch their heads over!

I took him back to the *tŷ hir*, shifted both of us back, and magicked us some food and drink – Kentucky fried chicken and chips, which he loves, and big bottles of fizzy mineral water to drink. Normally I'd have got coke, but (a) water would be better in a drought like this and (b) it would be better for his teeth. He went into it with both hands: from the look of him he hadn't eaten for a while, and for a leprechaun who dearly loves to eat, this must have been horrendous. When we'd both finished, I got rid of the debris – clean-picked bones and greasy red-and-white stripey cartons – and we both leaned back and looked at each other. His little pointed golden face was anxious.

'Right then, O'Liam,' I said, 'what on earth is going on?'

3

O'Liam burped. 'Ah, pardon, Lady. It has been a day or three since they fed me last and then it was only stale bread and water.'

'But what were you doing in there in the first place? What's happening, O'Liam? Where is everyone?'

'Well now. Where to begin…' He settled his small body more comfortably and folded his hands on his stomach. 'In the two years since you were last here, Lady –'

'TWO YEARS?' I said, flabbergasted. 'I haven't been away as long as that! Only a month at the most!'

'A month in your world, Lady. Here, it has been two years.'

I knew that time was different here – but somewhere along the line I had lost two years of my life! Good thing I was immortal, or I might start to panic.

'As I was saying, in the two years since you were here, things have changed.'

'I noticed,' I said dryly, looking around me.

O'Liam frowned. 'Will you ever let me finish speaking, woman?'

'Sorry. Go on, please.'

'For the first year everything was good, so it was. There was I, First Leprechaun to the Dragonking, and although he pined a wee bit when you left, he soon buckled down to it and started making a grand job of kinging it altogether. He made a fine lot of laws, and all of them fair, and held a court once a month where anyone with complaint or problem could come and talk to him face to face, and the people were happy and the land was prospering. And then – strange things started to happen.'

'Strange how?'

O'Liam scowled at me. 'Listen, and I'll tell you. Use them things one each side of your head that's for listening, and not the bit in the middle below that's for talking.'

'Sorry.' I could see that I would have to let him tell the tale at his own pace. And from past experience I knew that O'Liam wasn't able to make ANY story short! I sighed and let him get on with it.

'Well, now, what style of month is it now? April, May? About then.'

It was *spring?* The land looked as if it was September, after a long, hot, drought-ridden summer! I opened my mouth to say something, but O'Liam gave me a Hard Stare and I shut it again.

'Well, as I was saying, it was about six months ago, November, December, when we woke up in the middle of the night to find the whole sky going entirely mad. There was thunderbolts and lightning and big bangs and crashes and great flashes of light all over the place so that it was as light as day in the middle of the night. And then the rain started. It rained and rained until the rivers burst their banks and the little streams turned into big rivers, and the whole lot of them boiling and thrashing like they was trying to take over the universe. The village was flooded out, and all the villagers crowded into Castell Du, and your Aunt and Nest with them, and the rain didn't stop for seven days and seven nights.'

This was not Ynys Haf weather. Ynys Haf had *polite* weather. It didn't make a nuisance of itself.

'And no one could get out to tend their livestock, or their crops, or be about their business at all,' the little man continued, wiggling his green booted-feet. 'And just as we were starting to think the rain would never stop, it did. And the sun began. And it has been shining ever since. Not a drip nor a drop of rain has fallen on this land since the winter, and the damage that the rain did not do, the sun did. And when there was not a bit of food and hardly any water left in all the land for anyone to eat at all at all at all,' he said mournfully, 'and me being a person that needs to be fed on a regular basis it was entirely difficult, then, in the middle of the dark, dark night, they came.'

'They? Who? Who came?'

'If you'll listen, I'll tell you, Lady. Sure, and patience is not your virtue, is it?'

I bit my lip and shut up.

'It started with shouts and hollers to wake the dead, and arrows whizzing like wild things all over the place, and praise be the gatekeeper had remembered to shut the gate the night before, which is not a thing he does often, this being a peaceable style of place, for if he had not we would have been over-run and captured. Even the Dragonking.'

I sat forward, dying to ask questions.

'There was Rhiryd Goch and his brothers, and a great crowd of soldiers from the Lost Lands by their accents, and they had a great catapulty thing that fired boulders at the castle walls. Bad shots though, for they never quite got the range and just flattened a number of trees and a cow. We had only the villagers and a few soldiers, for Dragonking does not believe in war at all, and although I agree with him, there's no harm in being a little prepared.'

'Castell Du was under siege?'

'You have it exactly, Tan'ith. But that was not the worst of it, not at all.'

'*What?*' I was beginning to get really exasperated.

The leprechaun held up one finger and raised an eyebrow to shut me up. I wanted to smack him.

'Well, now,' he went on. 'Gwydion decided the only way to get us out of a sticky situation was to shape-shift the whole lot of us and get us out that way. So the whole lot of us were turned into a flock of starlings and we flew out of the castle early in the morning and headed for his other castle. What would the outlandish name of it be, now?'

'Castell y Ddraig,' I said, through gritted teeth. 'What happened next?'

'Well, now. When we turned up at Castell whatsisname, wasn't it full of soldiers from the Lost Land? All milling around and shooting arrows at us to keep us out. And to make matters worse there were some great savage creatures prowling around outside, hungry as lions and ten times as big, with teeth on them like carving knives and claws like claymores!'

I stared at him, wondering what on earth he was talking about. And then something clicked. THAT was what had troubled me when I'd been on the beach! I'd glanced into the cave where the Oldway creatures should have been. *They hadn't been there!*

'The Oldway creatures are loose?' I said,

incredulously. 'Who would be able to do that? It takes a powerful wizard even to allow them to move, let alone leave the sea-cave. And they're loose in Ynys Haf?'

O'Liam nodded solemnly. 'They are so. Wasn't that how I ended up in the dungeon all chained up and starved?'

'How?'

'One of the great ugly things had me cornered, my back to a rock, its great ugly slavering jaws coming closer and closer. I managed to get out by running beneath its body, but ran slap into the twins. And didn't they shut me up and leave me to rot, the nasty pair. They said they were going to send me somewhere, and I –'

'O'Liam,' I said carefully, 'I know I'm interrupting, but is Gwydion safe? And Aunty Fliss and Iestyn and Nest? Just tell me, please?'

'Oh, did I not say so? They are well, or were when I last was having a conversation with them. Oh yes, fit as fleas, and the villagers too.'

'Then where are they?'

'Hiding in the mountains, up in the North of the country, where it is at least cool. I think they are waiting for you.'

'Waiting for me? Why me?'

'Because you are the Lady, and Gwydion needs you to help him fight the invaders and take back his land. He cannot do it alone, Lady. He needs you.'

I had that 'who, me?' feeling again.

'Lady, I heard that Conor says you owe him a debt and none but you can repay it,' said O'Liam gingerly.

'Mm,' I said absent-mindedly, 'he sent me a note.'

'What debt might that be?' O'Liam asked.

'Well, I made a promise that I would give him Maebh, but without her magic,' I said. 'And he wants you back, O'Liam.'

The little man's golden, pointed face went a sickly, glowing white. I thought he would slither down the rock and faint. 'Me?' he said weakly. 'Conor wants me? Oh, mercy me, it will be the end of me. Is that where Ardwyn and Jason were going to send me? Back to Conor of the Land Beneath? Lady, you will not make me go back?'

'Oh, don't be silly, O'Liam. Just because Conor wants you back doesn't mean I'm going to send you. He says I stole you, but all I did was take you with me. It isn't as if he owns you, for goodness sake!'

The leprechaun's face was anguished. 'But he does, Lady! I belong to Conor, I am his and always will be. Little People are not free: we come of his blood and must do as he says. My Ma and Da were his, and my Grandma and Grand-da, and so am I, and so will my children be his.'

'But that's no better than slavery, O'Liam! No one has a right to own a human being! It isn't right!'

O'Liam smiled sadly. 'But I am not human, Lady. And as you are part human, part witch, you must understand the call of your different blood. I have no different blood. I am full leprechaun, and am tied to Conor until I die. Of course, it is much more comfortable to be tied to Conor with the Middlesome Sea between us, and much more convenient, so. But if he wants me back, then…'

'Then it's tough, because he can't have you,' I snapped. 'I'll sort out the Maebh problem somehow, but there is no way he is getting you back.'

'Sure, and I appreciate your sentiments, Lady,' O'Liam sighed, 'but if Conor of the Land Beneath wants me then sooner or later he will get me, I expect.'

'Over my dead body,' I said firmly. Then I crossed my fingers and hoped it wouldn't be necessary. 'Look, O'Liam, tomorrow I'm going North to find Gwydion and I really think you'd better come with me, especially if the Oldway creatures are lurking around here somewhere.'

'But of course I shall come with you!' His expression was utter amazement. 'I am Chief Leprechaun to the Dragonking of Ynys Haf – even if he is having a wee bit of trouble with his kingdom at the current time. My place is with him. And with you, Lady. Besides,' he said, a smile lighting his pointed face. 'If I run into one of them creatures again, sure and won't it be altogether a good idea to have a witch around to deal with it!'

From what I remembered of the Oldway creatures, I wasn't quite as confident. Once or twice the Oldway creatures had almost terminated me altogether! But that was then, this is now. I am the Lady, and much, much stronger than the novice witch who tangled with them last time.

4

'Ah, Lady dear!' O'Liam said sadly. 'I should have known that Lord Conor would not take the departure of me sitting down. Not only because of me, but because of the Maebh person.'

'What's Conor got to do with all this?'

'Oh, everything, Lady. Didn't he send thousands and thousands of his soldiers to find you, and when he couldn't find you his face was like a slapped backside, so it was, and his rage was terrible to behold.'

'Thousands of soldiers? Conor sent an *army* to find me?' I could hardly believe my ears.

The little man man nodded, sadly. 'And more, Lady. They attacked the Dragonking while he was sleeping, and wounded him, and chased off all the village people and –'

'Gwydion's *wounded?* He's hurt and you didn't tell me?" I grabbed the little man by his shirt-front and almost lifted him off the floor. He is very small and light as a feather, and even as I did it I felt VERY silly and a bit like Rambo.

'Sure, and didn't I just hear my own self right now doing just that?' O'Liam said, wriggling in my grasp. 'Would you put me down now, Lady, if you please?'

I dropped him. 'Where is he? How bad is he?'

'In the mountains, Lady. And he will recover, which means he is not dead, not in the slightest. Not even a little bit. At least, he wasn't when I last heard news, which was a day or so ago.'

'Take me to him, O'Liam,' I commanded. 'Do you know where he is?'

'I do so, Lady. But there's something el-'

It was too late. I had shifted him into a kestrel, and his words ended in a feeble squawk as he tried to make arms that had suddenly become wings do what he wanted. Then we took off and flew into the heat of the late afternoon, O'Liam flapping furiously.

The sky wasn't blue: it was too hot for that. It was a flat, coppery colour, as if the sun had singed the air. It became cooler as we flew into the mountains and a small breeze lifted my feathers and ruffled them.

I recognised the tall peaks and plunging valleys of Snowdonia: it looked odd to see it without the little train chugging up and down from the summit, and the great lakes that sat in the valleys looked like golden mirrors reflecting the uneasy sky.

It was into one of these valleys that O'Liam swooped, skimming down a steep escarpment, his long wings with their pale undersides almost touching the still water. He side-slipped along the small stream that fed the lake, following the trickle of clear water along the valley floor to where the mountain rose again, and the stream became a plunging waterfall.

And then he disappeared. One minute he was there, the next minute he was gone. I put on my brakes and looked wildly about to see where he'd gone. I could just make out the dark shadow of a cave behind the falls. Cautiously, I slipped behind the cool stream, and there was O'Liam.

I shifted him back. 'I thought I'd lost you for a minute.' I looked round at the dark, moist walls. 'Gwydion's here?' I shivered. 'This is a terrible place.'

'Sure and this is only the entrance hall, Lady,' O'Liam reassured me. 'Follow me.'

The little man trotted off towards the darkness at the back of the cave. I wished I had a torch. But then I remembered that I could command light when I needed it. *Moon*, I thought, *Moon, I need you!*

And there, obediently, it was, a small glowing ball suspended over our heads, bobbing ahead of us, shedding light so that we would not trip. As the tunnel grew lighter, the moon gradually faded, and when we reached daylight, it vanished.

At the end of the tunnel was a large, airy hollow, surrounded completely by steep green sides, as if someone had taken a spoon and hollowed out the mountain like a boiled egg. The sun shone down like molten copper, but here at least there was shade, and a few trees had seeded themselves somehow, and there was even a spring. Small leather tents had been erected here and there, but best of all there was no danger of being discovered unless the seeker could fly immediately overhead.

I looked about me, and instantly spotted Aunty Fliss. She was carrying a bowl, and looking worried.

'Flissy!' I called, and she swung round, her face breaking into a huge grin.

'Tansy!' she shrieked, dropped the bowl and ran towards me with her arms outstretched. We hugged, and then she spotted O'Liam, and he got the same treatment. The little man's golden face went a deep bronze colour with embarrassment.

'Ah, get off, woman!' he muttered. 'I can't find it in

myself to hug people on a Tuesday, no matter how much I like them.'

'Aunty Fliss, what's happening? Where's Gwydion? Is he all right?'

Flissy sighed and picked up the bowl. 'Gwydion's fine. At least, he will be. He'll be all the better for seeing you. At least, I hope he will. He's in a funny mood. Like a bear with a sore head. Or my Iestyn with a hangover. Come on, I'll take you to him.'

I followed her into one of the tents. Gwydion was lying propped up on a mattress. His arms were folded mutinously, and his face was like thunder. He didn't look up, so he didn't see me.

'If that's you, Fliss, I'm not taking any more of that disgusting medicine. My side is healing up and my leg is almost strong enough to walk on. If you really want me to get better, leave me alone.'

'Grouch!' I said, and at last he looked up. If I expected a smile I didn't get one.

'Oh. It's you. About time, too.'

'What?'

'Well, if you hadn't gone gallivanting all over Erin upsetting Conor of the Land Beneath we wouldn't be in this mess.'

I was so taken aback by his attitude I couldn't speak. I just opened and closed my mouth like a goldfish. At last I got my tongue back. 'And whose fault was it I was gallivanting all over Erin? Who went and got made a fool of by some little Irish dingbat who batted her eyelashes at him? Eh? Who got himself captured and enchanted? Wasn't me, was it, Gwydion? I wonder who that could have been?'

Gwydion muttered something I couldn't quite make out. O'Liam slithered out of the door of the tent, probably realising that he might get caught in the fall-out if one of us really blew up.

'What? Can't hear you. Speak up if you've got anything to say. Any excuses?'

'Oh, pay no attention to him, Tansy,' Aunty Fliss broke in. 'He's just fed up with being kept in bed, and angry because he can't be out and about doing things to get Ynys Haf back. But now you're here, and –'

'And nothing!' Gwydion bellowed. 'Who's Dragonking, eh? Me, not her! She's only going to be my Dragonqueen!'

'Oh, no I'm not!' I yelled back.

'Oh, yes you are,' he bawled.

'I'm not!'

'You ARE!'

'NOT!'

'ARE!'

'Oh, for goodness sake, you two!' Aunty Fliss had to yell to make herself heard. 'Will you stop it! Of course you're going to be Dragonqueen, Tansy, it's in the legend. And yes, of course you're Dragonking, Gwydion, but right now you're a wounded Dragonking, and if you don't stop being so horrible you WON'T GET ANY DINNER TONIGHT!'

That did it. I stared at Aunty Fliss's thunderous face and started to giggle. She stopped glaring at Gwydion and glared at me, instead, and then she started to chuckle. Gwydion scowled mutinously at both of us, and at last saw the funny side, and joined in.

O'Liam, hearing the howls of laughter, cautiously

poked his head round the tent door and decided it was safe to rejoin us. When we had all calmed down, and I had wiped the tears of laughter from my face, I went and gave Gwydion a hug. I would have given him a kiss, too, but there were too many people watching.

'Now,' I said. 'Will somebody please tell me what's been happening.'

It was a long story. It had begun when, late one night, Conor of the Land Beneath's soldiers had stolen across the drawbridge of Castell Du, and overpowered the gatekeeper (there were no sentries: Ynys Haf was at peace, after all). All might have been lost then and there, except that a certain little girl –

'– you remember her, Tansy,' Aunt Fliss said, 'Eifion Gwyn's little girl, Branwen. Red hair and freckles.'

Oh, I remembered Branwen. It had been Branwen whose good ideas had helped me last time.

Aunty Fliss explained how Branwen had been awake and on the battlements watching the moon. She had seen the shadowy shapes slither into the courtyard and had raised the alarm. But for her, the entire population of the castle might have been killed in their beds, because the soldiers were not mere leprechauns – they were rough, paid mercenary troops that Conor had recruited from far and wide.

The castle people had fought, but there were too many of the mercenaries and not enough weapons in the castle to fight properly.

'Merlin warned me Ynys Haf wouldn't always be at peace,' Gwydion said miserably. 'I thought he was just nagging for the sake of it. You know Merlin.'

I did. I still hadn't forgiven him for setting me up last time. 'Mm,' I said. 'Where is the old dear?'

Flissy sighed, exasperatedly. 'He took off with Taliesin again. King Arthur has got himself into a pickle in another Time, and accordingly to History Merlin has to be there. So he's been no help at all. Goodness knows when he'll be back, and he's bound to be in a foul temper anyway.'

'Why?' I knew I shouldn't have asked, but living history backwards is a bit confusing sometimes.

'Oh, he can't stand Guinevere. He says she's a flighty little miss and always has been, and if it was up to him he'd slap her bottom and send her somewhere to think about improving her behaviour.'

This wasn't quite my picture of Arthur's beautiful Queen. But hey, I'd never met her, had I?

'So, what happened next?'

'Well, Gwydion was wounded. He took an arrow in the side and when he fell down the stairs he broke his leg, so we took him out by the secret tunnel. And then when we got outside, we found a dragon in the tunnel opening, but luckily it was Bugsy.'

My head was spinning. 'Bugsy?'

'Gwydion's pet dragon, when he was a boy. He had to let it go when it got too big to sleep on his bed, but it turns up occasionally. You already met it once – the dragon that guarded Castell y Ddraig. Anyway, we lifted Gwyd onto his back and he led the way up here. This is his place.'

I looked around me, nervously. 'There's a dragon here?'

'Not right now. He's out hunting. He'll be back later.'

‘So,’ I said, ‘let me get this straight. You, Gwyd, and the whole village are holed up in the mountains – where’s Nest, Aunty Fliss?’

Flissy sighed. ‘Nest’s gone back to Erin, to try to reason with Conor of the Land Beneath. He’s winning, Tansy, and we can’t have that. She’s trying to find out what he wants, how we can make him stop.’

‘Oh, I know what he wants,’ I said grimly. ‘He wants O’Liam back, and he wants Maebh. And I’m not going to let him have either of them. He’d marmalise O’Liam if he could get his nasty little hands on him, and what he’s got planned for Maebh I don’t even want to think about. So, somehow or another, we’ve got to get out of this situation we’re in, recapture Castell y Ddraig, get rid of Conor’s soldiers, fix the weather, and convince Conor that he doesn’t want O’Liam or Maebh at all, really.’

Gwydion grinned. ‘And what will you do the day after tomorrow?’

I stuck my tongue out at him. ‘Oh, you’re so sharp you’ll cut yourself one day. Anything else I ought to know about? I don’t suppose anyone woke up the Great Druid?’ I was joking, honest.

‘The Great Druid’s still out of it, fortunately,’ Flissy said. ‘But the Oldway Creatures are loose …’

5

So it was true. The cave of the great stone Oldway Creatures was empty. Nothing but shadows and seaweed. I gulped. The thought of those ugly, savage monsters with their teeth and talons roaming around Ynys Haf was definitely the stuff of nightmares!

'So,' I said briskly, 'there's Conor to sort out, a couple of hundred rough soldiers – and the Oldway Creatures. Is that it, now?'

'Isn't that enough?' Gwydion was scowling again.

'More than enough, thank you very much.' I frowned at him. I had enough on my plate without having to argue with him as well. 'Look, Gwyd,' I began –

'If you're going to lecture me, you can shut up right now,' he said.

'All I was going to say,' I lied, rather fast, because I *had* been going to lecture him. 'is that O'Liam and I could really do with a drink and a rest before I even think about it. Right, O'Liam?'

'Oh, Lady, I could drink the Dubh Linh dry as bones, I could.'

After we'd had a long, cool herbal drink, Aunty Fliss found us some mattresses and we lay down in the shade of a tree. I didn't honestly expect to sleep, but I did. I awoke, startled, at the touch of a small hand on mine. It was evening, and kneeling beside me was a little girl with long plaits the colour of a marmalade cat and a crop of freckles like raisins in *bara brith.*

'Branwen!' I exclaimed in delight. 'Just the person

I wanted to see. I hear that if it hadn't been for you, Castell y Ddraig might have been lost!'

She blushed scarlet. 'My Dada said I ought to have been walloped because I had no business being out of bed that late, but Aunt Nest stopped him. She said if he walloped me, she'd wallop him. Don't see how she could, mind, her being little and a half-fairy, but I didn't get walloped, Lady.'

'Quite right too!' I said indignantly. 'The trouble with men in this Time is that occasionally they have to be put in their place, right?'

Branwen giggled. 'Right, Lady! Anyway, Lady, Aunt Flissy sent me to wake you. She said to tell you there's word from Erin.'

I was off the mattress like a jack-in-the-box. O'Liam was still snoring, so I didn't wake him. He'd had a fairly traumatic time of it, being stuck in a dungeon thinking his last hour was on its way. He probably needed his sleep.

With Branwen on my heels I headed for Gwydion's tent. The sun was going down, and the inside of the tent was dark. Aunty Fliss was setting rushlights in stands and lighting them, and the stink of the mutton-fat they were made from was overpowering.

'For goodness sake, Aunty Fliss, put them out,' I pleaded. 'We'll all choke to death.'

'But then we won't be able to see,' Gwydion said patiently, as if he was talking to an idiot. I was beginning to think that the hardest job I had to do was to get Gwydion back into a good temper!

Aunty Fliss put out the lights, and the shadows deepened. I pinned back the flap of the tent and waited for the moon to join us. It floated inside and hovered tidily up in the roof of the tent, looking like a Chinese lantern. Gwydion made no comment and I didn't even look his way.

'What's happened?' I asked. 'Branwen says there's news from Ireland.'

'Not good news,' Fliss said. 'Conor has captured Nest. He's holding her in the Land Beneath as security – until you take O'Liam back and give him Maebh.'

'That's not fair,' I protested. 'He can't do things like that.'

A small voice with an Irish accent spoke from the open tent doorway. 'Ah, Lady, but he can. He is Conor, Lord of the Land Beneath, and he wants what is his. There is only one thing a Leprechaun hates more than losing his possessions, and that's his dignity getting a hammering. And you've done both.'

'I never touched his dignity!' I said.

'Ah, but you did. You took back your friend, Lady Haf, you helped me escape and you made him a promise concerning Maebh. Until you keep that promise, his dignity is in terrible, awful pain, believe me.'

Aunty Fliss was looking at the little man, and there was pity on her face. 'There is more, O'Liam, dear,' she said softly.

He was silent for a moment, and then he whispered, 'What?'

'Conor also has a friend of yours.'

The little man's voice was quieter still. 'Who?'

'Siobhan Flowerface.'

O'Liam's mouth twisted. He took a deep breath and

closed his eyes before he spoke, and his voice was barely audible. 'Then I must go back, and go now.'

'Who's Siobhan Flowerface?' I asked.

'Can't you guess?' Flissy said. 'His girlfriend.'

'You've got a girlfriend, O'Liam?' I don't know why I was surprised: he was quite good-looking, if rather short.

'I have so. And it was in my mind to ask permission of the Dragonking to go back to the Land Beneath one day soon. If I could not bargain for her, which certainly I could not, perhaps I could steal her away from Conor somehow. But he knows me too well, and he has struck me where the wound will be mortal. I miss her entirely, Lady, and my life is nothing without her.'

'If you're going back, O'Liam,' I said fiercely, 'then I'm going back with you.'

'And then Conor would have the two of us, and we'd be not at all better off,' he said sadly. 'And Siobhan would be a widow before she's a wife.'

'Not if Conor doesn't know we're there,' I argued.

'Conor knows everything,' he said.

'Oh no, he doesn't. He didn't know I was going to take T.A. away, and he certainly didn't know I was going to shift you and take you as well, did he? Otherwise he'd have sealed the exits from the Land Beneath long before we got to them, right?'

Hope stirred in the little man's eyes. 'You could be right at that, Lady. Perhaps there is a chance –'

'There's every chance, O'Liam. We can beat him. Are you with me, O'Liam of the Green Boots?'

'Is cuma le fear na mbróg cá leagann sé a chos,' he said, and grinned.

'Pardon?' Gwydion and I spoke together.

'We have a saying for it,' O'Liam said, raising one emerald-booted foot in the air, '"The man with the boots does not mind where he places his foot". And where Siobhan is concerned, my boots and the feet inside them and the glorious shiny socks on the toeses is entirely not minding at all.'

For once one of O'Liam's sayings had come out right! 'First light tomorrow, we leave,' I said. 'But right now I'm starving!'

O'Liam was, too, and I noticed that even Gwydion did justice to the Big Macs and fries I produced, and helped himself to a large lump of my pepperoni pizza. At least we managed to eat some of it before the night got complicated…

And oh, it did get complicated. Naturally, even in a natural hideaway like this one, guards had been posted, and we were just squabbling over the last french fry when we heard shouting outside. Flissy stuck her head out of the tent to see what was going on. She turned, her face white.

'Quick, Gwydion,' she said, 'if you can stand up and move, get ready to do it now!'

'Why?'

'Oldway Creature,' she said, and darted out of the tent. My stomach churned and I thought I might lose my pizza – the bit I'd eaten, I mean – in what Heledd's husband Siôn calls 'a technicolour yawn' if you get my meaning. I was scared. Nevertheless, I forced down the bit of crust I was munching and followed Flissy outside.

The Creature was bigger than I'd remembered: perhaps they were older and had grown – I had, after all. This one was about twelve metres tall, and not a pretty sight. O'Liam stuck his head out of the tent and then pulled it back in again, fast. His voice squeaked with terror behind me.

'Oh, it's a monster, Dragonking, and I'd advise you to take a good look at the stars when it eats the tent, for certain them's the last stars you'll ever see in your whole natural life!' he babbled. 'Oh, we're all going to die, we are so!'

'Shut up, O'Liam,' Gwydion growled, 'and get out of my way.'

I glanced behind me: Gwydion was in the doorway of the tent, standing up, favouring one leg, clutching his side with one hand, his sword in the other, ready to do battle with the vast, leathery nightmare that was bearing down on us.

As for me, my brain had gone completely blank. It does this to me at times of great terror, and this was certainly one of those. It was the look of the thing, the great muscular forearms tipped with talons that shone in the moonlight; the mighty back legs that thudded on the ground; the long, scaly tail that swept around behind it, knocking people off their feet and tents from their moorings. And the eyes: small, yellow, with odd, misshapen pupils like a lizard's eyes, and the teeth. Oh, the teeth! Even my dentist-from-hell would have quailed at the sight of these gnashers. Each tooth was as long as a banana – only much, much sharper. If you can imagine a banana crossed with a razor, you might have about one-tenth of the idea … Its breath wasn't much cop, either; it definitely wasn't using dental floss. And the fact that I could smell it meant that I was far too close for comfort.

I racked my brains for ideas and came up with nothing. A big, fat zero. I hurled a spell at it, but it bounced harmlessly off the iron-hard plates of its chest. It reared up over me and Gwydion, and roared. Then my brain clicked into gear and I remembered what I'd done last time: I'd used the tiny sprigs of the Lady's magical staff, the wonderful bush that had held buds, fruit and flowers all at the same time. But now I was the Lady – and the one thing the Lady hadn't given me was her staff! So now what did I do?

A small, cool voice spoke in my brain. *'You don't need the staff, Tan'ith. All the trees in Ynys Haf are magical – use your brain, dimwit!'*

Was it the Lady – the Lady-who-had-been – speaking to me? My brain, which had sort of gone walkabout, clicked back into place. In a flash I shape-shifted into an owl, swooped past the creature's gaping jaws, and into the nearest bush: it was an elder, the great sprays of white flowers protected from the merciless sun by the mountains, and still fresh. I ripped a beakful of blossom from the bush, and launched myself at the Creature. I hovered over it, silently, but the movement of my wings caught its attention, and it reared up, slashing with its talons, trying to rip me out of the sky. I went in under the swiping sharpness and placed the white elderflowers neatly on the Oldway Creature's shoulder. Instantly it shuddered and turned to stone. The danger was over. One down, five to go.

I landed, shifted back, and closed my eyes in relief. *Thanks, Lady,* I thought. *You saved our lives.*

But there was no reply.

Aunty Fliss emerged from behind a tree and, hands on hips, surveyed the stone monster. 'That was a close thing, Tanz,' she remarked. 'Well done.'

'We'd have been finished if the Lady hadn't helped me, Aunty Fliss,' I confessed. 'She helped me.'

Aunty Fliss looked at me strangely. 'She couldn't have, Tanz. There is no Lady except you, any more. *You* are the Lady.'

Come to think of it, I couldn't ever remember the Lady using words like 'dimwit'. But I knew what I'd heard, and I didn't think it had been my own voice. I opened my mouth to argue, but Aunty Fliss was staring over my shoulder. I was almost scared to turn round in case another Oldway Creature had found its way behind the waterfall. I got ready to shift and head for the nearest tree. I turned round.

There, looking decidedly smug, was –

6

'What are you doing here?' I said.

T.A. grinned. 'The Ant had second thoughts,' she said gleefully. 'She decided you needed me after all.'

I frowned. 'Well, I'm glad to see you and all that, but things are going to get pretty hairy round here and I really think it's probably going to be too –' She wasn't listening.

'Gwydion! Are you all right? You look awful!' She rushed past me and put her arms round Gwydion's middle. She couldn't reach any higher. He gave her a hug, I noticed, and a big grin, which was more than I'd got.

'I'm fine,' he said nonchalantly. 'It was only a flesh wound and a broken leg.'

'Only a flesh w –'

'*As* I was saying,' I went on, 'I think it would be better if you –'

'It was nothing, honestly, I'll be fine in a couple of days.'

'With Fliss looking after you, I expect you will.'

My friend let go of Gwydion's middle and turned to the leprechaun. 'O'Liam dear, whatever's wrong?'

'Oh, Lady Haf, am I not the saddest soul in the whole, entire, round world? Sure and hasn't Conor of the Land Beneath gone and stole my one true love?'

'Oh, no!' T.A. breathed sympathetically. 'Poor you! But don't worry, O.'Liam, we'll rescue her for you. Won't we, Tanz?'

'No,' I said crossly. Who was the Lady around here? '*We* won't. You're going back, right now.'

'Oh, no, I'm not,' T.A. said. 'Aunt Ant said you'd say that, and she said to tell you that she and your Mam have scryed the future and there isn't any danger – to me, at least – so they said I should come to keep you from making any really big mistakes.' So there, her expression said, but she didn't. Then she spotted the stone Creature. 'Good grief, look at that ugly thing,' she remarked, walking all round it. 'Hi, Aunty Fliss. That's a seriously weird statue to have in your camp!'

'Don't you recognise it, T.A.?' I said crossly. 'Haven't you seen it somewhere before?'

'Well, it looks a bit like an Oldway Creature,' she said, 'but that's impossible, isn't it? They're all down in the cave below Castell Du, right?'

'Wrong,' I said. 'Conor has loosed them, and they're all over the place. Which is why I think it would be a really good idea to find a Time Door and get you out of here, fast.'

'No,' T.A. said, and that, apparently, was that, because she gave Aunty Fliss a hug and then the two of them shepherded Gwydion back into his tent. And left me and O'Liam outside, him sighing, me fuming.

'I think,' O'Liam said carefully, 'it's a case of what you can't change you must get on with, so.'

'I wish,' I said bitterly, 'that I could work out exactly who is in charge round here. I thought I was the Lady.'

'And I,' said a voice from the tent, 'am Dragonking.'

I went in. T.A. was sitting cross-legged on the end of Gwydion's mattress, and he was looking far happier than he had when I'd arrived.

'But you aren't fit to do anything, Gwydion,' I said patiently. 'Looks like it's up to me, doesn't it? Just the way it was last time.'

'I'm getting better every day,' Gwydion retorted. 'Give me a week and I'll be able to come with you.'

I opened my mouth, but Aunty Fliss got there first. 'They haven't got a week, Gwydion dear,' she said. 'They have to go now. Conor won't wait. Tanith has to make him stop all this and be sensible, otherwise it will just go on getting worse. You get well, and then you can join them in Ireland, if they aren't back by then.'

Gwydion wasn't happy, but then, he wasn't fit, either. His broken leg was almost healed, though still weak, but the wound in his side had been anything but a 'flesh wound'. Fliss changed his dressings three times a day, and when I saw the healing scar I was horrified. 'That's awful!' I whispered. 'Oh, Gwydion, was it bad?'

'We almost lost him,' Flissy said merrily, smearing the wound with honey, 'but thanks to Nest he's still around.'

My knees felt weak at the thought of it, and I wanted to give him the hug I'd not been allowed to give, yet. But there were still too many people around, and besides, Gwydion was ratty because he wasn't allowed to go with us. With strict instructions to stay away from Oldway creatures – I left Nest a Branch just in case – we were off. O'Liam, T.A. and I shifted into golden eagles – well, we were half-way up Snowdon, right? – and soared up out of the mountain hideaway, heading for the coast.

It was wonderful being an eagle: I'd never been one before, but the pure joy of those mighty wings, the splayed primary feathers fingering the air to balance me on the up-currents that rushed from the valleys into the mountains, the ecstasy of tumbling out of a thick bank of cloud to see Ynys Môn in front of us, the utter power of the greatest bird ever to soar over Wales! Even the horrors of the drought-stricken countryside below me couldn't entirely dampen my spirits, although O'Liam seemed to be having a bit of difficulty flying the right way up at times. Apparently if he concentrated too hard on flapping his wings, he lost his balance and flipped over.

We hurtled over Aberffraw, where the Princes of Gwynedd would one day have their summer palace on the shore, followed the coast up to Holy Island, swooped down and perched on the rocky shore at the edge of the Irish Sea – or what O'Liam referred to as the Middlesome Sea, it being sort of middlesome to everywhere, as far as he was concerned.

Last time, we had made landfall near Wicklow by my reckoning, although I hadn't had an idea of that at the time. It was only by looking at a map when I got back to my Time that I'd worked it out. This time I decided that we'd land near Drogheda and approach Conor of the Land Beneath on a fairly roundabout way. We didn't want to march right up to his front door and get in his face now, did we?

I shifted us back. O'Liam hopped and shuffled,

trying to get the feel of his arms and legs. It's hard to describe what it's like shape-shifting to someone who hasn't ever done it, but the first couple of times someone is shifted it's a bit like – oh, I don't know. Sniffing fizzy cola up your nose and trying to squeeze your whole body into one leg of a very tight pair of jeans. Sort of. And that doesn't do it justice.

'I suppose we'd better go and find someone with a boat to take us across,' T.A. suggested.

I shook my head. 'You've got to be joking, T.A. I don't do boats, remember?'

T.A. shrugged. 'If you're afraid you're going to be sick, I think you're worrying unnecessarily. The sea's like a mill-pond, look.'

She thought she had me, but she was wrong. I'd been thinking about this problem since it had dawned on me that crossing to Ireland was a horrible possibility. Like I said, I don't do boats. I smirked. 'Ah, but do seals drown, T.A.?'

O'Liam's eyes went very big and round. 'What, me swim all the way across the Middlesome Sea? Oh, I don't like the swimmit thing at all, Lady! All cold and wet and drowny it is. Oh, please, let's take a boat like ordinary leprechauns do?'

'It's different when you're a seal, O'Liam,' I reassured him. 'You didn't do flying, either, until I shifted you, did you? Did you like being an eagle?'

He frowned, suspiciously. 'I did so, once I got used to the winds being such terrible bullies and the upsomeness of it turning me the wrong way altogether.'

'Being a seal will be just as much fun, trust me.'

'Ah, Lady. I trust you. And isn't that the pity of it

when – aaaark?' His faintly panic-stricken golden eyes looked back at me from the dog-like, inquisitive face of a large grey seal.

'There,' I said, 'you just sit there, O'Liam, and get used to your flippers while I shift T.A. and me.'

When we were ready, the three of us flopped to the edge of the water and plunged in. Well, two of us did. T.A. and I had gone about 200 metres out to sea before we realised O'Liam wasn't with us. Back we went. O'Liam was at the water's edge, and his seal-face was utterly panic-stricken.

'Look, O'Liam, it's dead easy!' I barked.

'Come on in, the water's lovely,' T.A. added, spinning herself like a corkscrew in the clear water. O'Liam sat on the seaweed and shook his head. His huge eyes filled up with tears.

We coaxed and pleaded for ages. Then I had an idea. I left T.A. arguing with the leprechaun, swam out and kept looking until I found a large, fat fish. A flurry, a swirl of water, and it was held firmly between my jaws, and I could taste the delicious tang of its salty, slimy, fishy scales. I swam back to the beach, and put my head out of the water. O'Liam spotted the fish, and since it was about 90% seal and only 10% O'Liam, and since O'Liam is exceedingly fond of fish anyway, the lure of a fine, fat fish was altogether too much. O'Liam was flopping through the shallows after me. Once he was deep enough, I handed – well, mouthed – over the fish. It was gone in a second. O'Liam wiped his whiskers with his flipper.

'There,' I said. 'You're swimming beautifully, O'Liam. Come on, let's go.'

With a bark of panic O'Liam sank like a stone and, quite expertly, began to drown.

'Oh, good grief,' I muttered, and T.A. and I got our noses and flippers under the leprechaun and shoved him back to the surface. 'Can't you swim, O'Liam?'

The seal shook his head. 'Leprechauns don't,' he spluttered back. 'Leprechauns drown.' And he did his very best to do exactly that all over again, blowing streams of bubbles as he disappeared beneath the waves.

What could I do? I gave in, magicked a boat, changed the leprechaun back and we shoved him on board quick, before he sank for the third time. 'Do you want to ride or swim, T.A.?' I asked, resignedly.

'Swim of course! You don't honestly think I'd pass up a chance to be a seal, do you?'

So we took it in turns to tow O'Liam by the rope attached to the bow of the little boat, while the other one swam, twirled, danced, spun, flew through the water, played with passing dolphins and generally had a (sorry, pun coming up) whale of a time. Meanwhile O'Liam lay on the bottom of the boat, shivering like a wet cat, sneezing pathetically and coughing up sea water. Half way across, the wind got up and he started to get sea-sick. His golden face turned as green as his boots, and O'Liam throwing up wasn't too much fun for T.A. who happened to be towing him at the time. We pointed him to the back of the boat and it was better after that.

It was a long swim, but we arrowed through the water in fine style, and by half way through the afternoon the coast of Ireland was in sight, and very soon the cluster of tiny white-washed stone cottages that was Drogheda appeared ahead of us.

We bobbed beside the boat, looking.

'Do you think there'll be a Guardian, Tanz?' T.A. whispered.

'Of course there will be,' O'Liam said. The wind had dropped, and the sight of his homeland seemed to have cheered him up. 'There is always a Guardian. The question is, what style of a Guardian?'

'You mean it might be a Big Deirdre?' I whiffled, my whiskers twitching nervously.

'Oh, no. Big Deirdre's down to the south of here, she is, and there is only one of her. Guardians don't move about from port to port like gypsies, so. If you'll give me a minute to think, maybe I can remember who guards Drogheda.'

At least he'd said 'who', not 'what'. I found that sort of comforting.

His face brightened. 'Ah! Got it! If I remember rightly, it's the Cavan Banshee got the job when it was advertised.'

'B-b-banshee?' T.A. and I said together. 'There's no such thing as a banshee –'

But of course, this was Erin, and there was.

7

'Nothing much to be scared of in a Banshee, right?' T.A. said nervously. 'All they do is scream, isn't it?'

'Ah, but,' O'Liam said mournfully clutching the sides of the boat, 'when a banshee screams the scarlet blood will freeze solid in your veins at the sound.'

'We could put cotton-wool in our ears,' T.A. suggested. 'Then we wouldn't hear it.'

'Oh, you'd hear it,' the leprechaun said firmly. 'When a banshee screams, her voice will penetrate six feet of earth, kill all the worms and waken up the dead. Except, of course, they aren't dead until she screams.'

'Pardon? What do you mean, "they aren't dead until she screams"?' I didn't like the sound of this much.

'Isn't that why banshees scream? It's a warning: they're letting folk know in advance when death is just around the corner.'

'But if it's a warning, couldn't the person just avoid it? Go elsewhere or something?'

'Ah, well. Our elders have thought about the problem of banshees long and hard,' O'Liam said. 'Does the chicken go before the cart, or is it the horse first before the egg?'

'Pardon?' T.A. and I said together.

'Turn your thinking bits to this wee puzzle,' said O'Liam. 'Is the banshee's scream just telling you that death is coming, or does she bring it with her? By the time you've heard her scream, is it too late? Or is it not altogether too late entirely? Who can tell? But speaking for myself I do not want to be around at all when death arrives, for whenever it finds me it will be entirely too soon for me.'

'I'll second that,' T.A. muttered. 'The question is, what can we do about it? I know. We'll shift into birds and fly past her.'

O'Liam shook his head. 'She'd know you weren't birds, and also, creatures die as often as mortals – but only the once each, of course. And she'll surely see you going overhead, or trotting past in a fur coat, or wriggling in the earth beneath her toeses, and she'll scream and scream and – well, and then there's death, just where you didn't want to meet him.'

I had a thought. 'But if the banshee can't scream, then nobody dies, right?'

'You are right, so,' O'Liam agreed.

'Then all we have to do is stop her screaming!'

'And how is it that you propose to do that?' The little man put his head on one side and twiddled his thumbs.

'Jump on her from behind, grab her, tie her up and gag her?' T.A. suggested.

'By the time you'd laid a finger upon her she'd be screaming fit to burst. And you cannot lay a finger on a banshee, because they do not have bodies to lay fingers upon at all.'

'How can it not have a body? It needs a body to scream. And do you mean we won't be able to see it, either?' I asked.

'Oh, you'll see her. Ooooh, Lady, the pale, ghostly, ghastly, terrible, awful sight of a banshee is enough to make you quake in your boots. There are those that have died entirely from fright at the first look of her.

She's made of mists and moonshine, and she flooters about you in an altogether unnatural type of way. But you cannot touch her. Your hands would go right through. Unless it's a Tuesday, of course. On Tuesdays even banshees have to eat.'

'T.A.,' I said suddenly, 'what's today?'

T.A. screwed up her whiskery face and counted on her flippers. 'Tuesday.'

'Got it!' I said triumphantly. 'Gotitgotitgotit!'

T.A. whiffled her whiskers at me. 'What?' she barked.

'Can you think of something that, when you eat it, you can't possibly *speak*, let alone scream?'

T.A. frowned, and thought, and then corkscrewed in the water, splashing joyfully. 'Oh, yes, Tanz! I think I'm with you! Aunty Dwina's treacle toffee!'

'Exactly!' I crowed. 'Just as soon as the banshee opens her mouth to scream, we chuck in the treacle toffee and Bob's your uncle.'

'Do you have an Uncle Bob, T.A.?' O'Liam enquired interestedly. 'Wasn't I telling the Lady here just the other day that I do not have an Uncle Bob although she was under the impression that I have. Well, I don't, of course, although I have a –'

'I remember, O'Liam,' I said hurriedly, not wanting the leprechaun to climb his family tree.

T.A. and I towed the little boat up on to the sandy beach, and then I shifted us back. O'Liam climbed stiffly out, and stood shivering. He was a sad sight: his clothes were soaked and his green boots – well, he'd been horribly sick, and honestly, you don't want to know about the green boots, not really.

I magicked him a change of clothing, and a fresh pair of green boots. I also got him a new pair of socks, because I don't think he'd changed his lurex ones since I gave them to him, and to put it mildly, they were not sweet company.

Once T.A. and I were comfortable in soft leather trousers and tunics, we set off across the sand and pebbles and up the winding road to the beach.

'I just hope the banshee doesn't see us before we see her,' T.A. muttered. 'Or hear us, or smell us, or –'

'I get the picture, T.A..'

'I could go ahead and take a wee look,' O'Liam suggested. 'But if it's any help a banshee has to look you in the face before she screams at you, or it doesn't count.'

'But what if she sees you?'

'Leprechauns are not seen if they do not want to be. Even by banshees.'

'Are you saying that it's only us that's in danger of getting screamed at, O'Liam?' I stared at him.

'Oh, not at all. For while she's screaming at you two, I shall be screamed at also as well, because I shall be there.'

'But there's no reason for you to be there if you can get past her without any trouble.'

The leprechaun frowned and pulled himself up to his full height (about four feet tall on tiptoe). 'Lady, I am Leprechaun-in-Chief to the Dragonking of Ynys Haf. Would I abandon his Dragonqueen in her time of peril? I would not, so, and it is wrong of you to think that I would.'

'Well, I still think it would be a good idea if you

made yourself scarce while we get past. Then if we get screamed at, you can go back and tell Gwydion what happened to us.'

'Ah, now that's a sound idea, Lady,' the little man said. 'Now that's worth considering, so it is!'

But all the same, when we came face to face with the banshee, O'Liam was with us. He'd gone on ahead, running in his leprechaun way from place to place like a freeze-frame-fast-forward video. He'd flicker to hide behind a rock, and then freeze behind it, then flicker somewhere else. He'd been gone about three minutes when suddenly he hurtled round a rock and skidded to a halt in front of us.

'She's up ahead, and she's cheating, so she is. She's in a big old oak on the left of the path. And she's a terrible efficient style of banshee – her mouth's entirely too big for the rest of her.'

'All you have to do is tell us when she opens her mouth to scream. Up a tree, is she? How far ahead?'

'Oh, a dozen and a half paces. A dozen, ten, nine – oh, there she is, there she is.' The little man winked out and wasn't there any more. I hope he had his fingers in his ears!

'Don't look at her, T.A.,' I muttered, magicking a huge lump of Aunty Dwina's special treacle toffee into my hand.

Something flickered at the edge of my vision. Something pale and smoky, with coldness pouring off it like mist off a mountain. I got this TERRIBLE URGE to turn and look at it. Suddenly a voice squeaked in my ear, 'Her mouth is as open as the Cave of Cashel, Tan'ith! And oh, oh, she's taking a deep breath!'

Instantly I turned, and chucked the treacle toffee into the huge, open mouth of the banshee. The thing about this particular sort of toffee is that it is soft and chewy, and the flavour is so wonderful that you taste it instantly it hits your tongue. The banshee clamped her jaws on the lump of sweet stuff, and immediately got the chewies. Her greenish pale face screwed up. I don't know if anyone else in the whole world has ever seen a banshee smile, but we did. She stopped tearing her misty hair, stopped hovering in mid air in the shade of the tree, came down to earth with a surprisingly solid thump for a wraith, and started to chew. And dribble. It was a very large lump of toffee.

'Quick!' I yelled, and T.A. and I shot past her, heads up, feet going like Olympic sprinters, our fingers in our ears just in case, but the only sound that came from the banshee was a contented chewy sort of slurp. We didn't stop running, mind, until we were well out of earshot, and heading up a steep hill. At the top, we stopped and looked back. In the distance we could see the banshee, sitting contentedly beside the road. She was probably still chewing.

O'Liam suddenly flickered back into view beside us. 'Will you look at that, now!' he marvelled. 'What amazing stuff that must be, to have such a calming effect on a nervous type of thing like a banshee.' He cocked his head and glanced up at me. 'I can't help wondering what a bit of that stuff might taste like. Would it be dangerous at all?'

I could take a hint as well as the next person. I magicked a big bag and we joined the banshee in the delights of treacle toffee. Not only was it totally delicious (magical versions of food are always better than the originals, and Aunty Dwina's toffee was magical to start with) it also kept O'Liam silent for the best part of twenty minutes, which had to be good.

'Well,' T.A. said when her jaws were free. 'We made it past the guardian of the port. As long as we don't run into Big Deirdre on the rampage, we should be all right from now on.'

O'Liam tried to speak, but his jaws weren't unstuck yet.

'I've been thinking about Big Deirdre,' I said, idly kicking a stone along the path. 'I think we should try to get her on our side.'

'Tanz, you have got to be joking! From what you and Nest said, Big Deirdre is someone to stay well away from, right?'

'Normally, yes. But O'Liam said something that's made me think.'

O'Liam's eyes were bulging with the effort of not being able to speak. To be fair, I *had* given him the biggest lump of toffee!

'Careful, Tanz, T.A. said seriously. 'You don't think very often. You might overtax your brain. The whole thing might blow up!'

'Ha, ha, very funny. Not,' I pulled a face at her. 'Pay attention, T.A. O'Liam said that Conor of the Land Beneath had hunted down Deirdre's baby and killed it. He had its head stuffed and mounted on the wall of his trophy room. Deirdre hates all leprechauns, but especially Conor. It would make sense if we could get her on our side, right?'

'Oh, definitely. But how are you going to get close enough to a rampaging giant to talk her into it?'

'Oh, I'll think of something. If we run into her.'

O'Liam's mouth was empty at last. 'Oh, Lady, if there's one type of person you cannot trust more than a leprechaun, it's a shifting giant, so. And Deirdre being the female sort, she's sneakier than anything. Oh, Lady, don't even try to get Big Deirdre on your side!'

'We'll see how things turn out, O'Liam. Now, is there anything else around here I ought to know about before it screams at us, or eats us, or treads on us?'

O'Liam wiped a dribble of toffee off his chin. 'Where would you like me to begin, Lady? Will I start with the Pwca Horse and go on to the Great Worm of Mullingar, or will I tell you about the Terrible Beast of Loch Ree first? Or shall I mention to you the Awful Black Dog of Tullamore and the Howling Spirits of Arvagh, and –'

'Oh, crumbs, O'Liam, enough already! I don't think I can cope with any more on an empty stomach. The banshee was bad enough!'

'Oh, now. Is your stomach empty? Then certainly we must stop and eat, we must indeed.'

8

So we found a place in the shadow of some trees, with a small stream wandering past us, and I magicked us some goodies. O'Liam ate jacket potatoes crammed with butter and cheese, for the very first time, and he ate the lot, including the skins, which in my opinion is the best bit. Then, when we were full as eggs, I 'found' some sleeping bags in thin air and we snuggled down for the night.

The dew was on us when we woke, and I couldn't remember stirring at all the whole night through. T.A. and I washed the sleep out of our eyes in the icy stream, but O'Liam dipped in a finger and shuddered.

'All this washing! It's no good, no good at all. You'll wear your skins out, so you will, and then where will you be? All bare entirely and the bones of you fraying at the edges and likely dropping off!'

Well, I let him get away with not washing just the once, but if we were going to be together for any length of time, sooner or later he was going to have to grit his teeth and bear it!

When we'd eaten breakfast (bacon butties all round) and were all packed up and ready to go, I fixed O'Liam with a Hard Stare. 'Right, O'Liam, what about all these creatures you were trying to scare us with last night? What was it, the Pwca horse? A Great Worm? You were winding us up, right?'

'Well, and isn't that exactly what the Great Worm does, Lady! It winds you up in its nasty scaly coils and squeeeeeezes you and squeeeeeezes you until your eyes pop out, so it does. And then it takes a tiny wee nibble of the top of your head, just to finish you off before it eats you up altogether, skin and bones and teeth and all.'

'You're joking!' I stared at the little man.

'Well, just a wee bit. It doesn't eat you all entirely. It always spits out the head of you, because it crunches and the bony bits stick in its teeth and it can't bear that at all, not at all.'

T.A. had gone pale. 'He isn't joking, Tanz. He means it.'

'And what about all the other stuff?'

'The Pwca, and the Beast of Loch Ree, and the Black Dog of Tullamore and the Howling Spirits of Arvagh? Oh, yes. Then there's the Hounds of the Morrigan, and the Wailing Hag of Ballinallack. Nasty bit of countryside round here. We don't often come here, to tell you the truth. Oh, and then there's the –'

'Why exactly are we here, O'Liam?' I think my teeth were gritted, because my voice sounded funny. 'Why did we land at Drogheda when there's all these things waiting for us?'

He stared at me. 'It wasn't my idea, Lady! "We'll go in at Drogheda", you said, and so we did!'

'Why didn't you warn me?' I knew what he was going to say. 'I know, don't say it, O'Liam. I didn't ask, did I?' I'd forgotten that Leprechauns are basically sneaky, and that includes not giving away information unless it's asked for. 'But I would have thought that you wouldn't want to run into any of that stuff any more than we would!'

'Oh, I don't. But didn't I mention that leprechauns don't get seen unless we want to be seen?'

'You did indeed, O'Liam.'

'Shall we set off now?' he asked politely. 'I'm a wee bit anxious to see Siobhan Flowerface, and I wouldn't say no to looking in on my old Mammy, neither.'

'Your Mammy?' I said, faintly. 'You have a Mammy?'

'Ah, to be sure I have. Doesn't everybody?'

'How far is it to the Land Beneath?'

O'Liam pointed down. 'We're here already, Lady.'

'We are?'

'Of course. As soon as we left the causeway and passed the Banshee, we were walking over Conor's Land.'

'So we don't need to shift and fly?'

'Not unless you want to, Lady, though it might be quicker if we did.'

'But I thought you said we were at the Land Beneath already!'

'We are, so. But the Land Beneath stretches all over Erin, and Conor's palace is closer to Wicklow than it is to Drogheda.'

'So we'd better fly then.'

'We'd most certainly get there all the quicker if we did.'

'Are we going directly to Conor's palace, Tanz?' T.A. asked.

I sneaked a look at O'Liam: he was trying to fold up his cosy sleeping bag so that he could take it with him. I whispered urgently to TA: 'I think it would be a good idea if we tried to find Big Deirdre and get her on our side, first. We need all the help we can get.'

'What about the old guy who helped you last time? Couldn't he help?'

'The Hermit of Glendalough? Poor old soul, I think he'd have difficulty walking across the room without falling asleep. No, he's no good.'

I'd forgotten that leprechauns have ears like a bat's.

'If it's Big Deirdre you're looking for, then we'd better get a move on. But why we didn't come through her port instead of coming the long way round escapes me entirely.'

'If we'd come through her port she'd probably have killed us before we had a chance to talk to her. No, I want to sneak up on her, not the other way about. Are you ready?'

I don't know what made me do it: I shifted us all into magpies. We were incredibly handsome birds with our iridescent blue feathers glinting on our wings, but a magpie wasn't a pleasant bird to be inside, somehow. Although the brain is mainly me, whenever I shape-shift there has to be a part of the whole that is the creature itself: otherwise I would be me in a magpie's feathers, but without the faintest idea of how to fly. Magpies, I discovered, have a little nugget of pure wickedness inside them; they are constantly looking for mischief. They are very efficient flying machines, though, and we sped through the warm air towards Wicklow.

We'd been flying for about half an hour when I looped back to have a word with T.A. – and did a double-take. Unseen by any of us, a fourth magpie had tagged along.

'T.A.,' I whispered, 'I think we're being followed.'

'What?'

'There's another magpie following us. Maybe he fancies you!'

She looked over her shoulder. 'Should we talk to him?'

'How do you know it's a him?'

'I don't. Maybe it's a she, and she's lonely.' I'd never spoken to a wild creature before – unless it was a wild creature I'd shifted one of my friends into!

I dropped back still further, until I was flying alongside the stranger. 'Lovely day, isn't it?' I said. Look, I know it was dumb, but what else do you say to a bird? *What's your opinion on the cultural and political situation in Outer Mongolia?* I don't think so, somehow. *Worms are juicy this year?* Well, OK. Maybe that *would* have made more sense. But anyway, the magpie gave a startled squawk and fell out of the sky.

'Was it something I said?' I asked T.A., and she chuckled.

'Had I better go and see if it's all right?'

'If you can do it without terrifying it out of its life, poor thing!'

So I went into a dive, and swooped down to where the other magpie had disappeared. I looked and looked, but I couldn't see the bird. I was about to rejoin T.A. and O'Liam, who were getting quite far away by now, when a movement caught my eye.

It was a girl, running. She was small, and her hair was as black as night, and she was so pretty that I wanted to smack her. She had lifted her skirts up around her knees and was sprinting as fast as her legs would carry her towards a castle on a small hill.

Maebh!

I was horribly undecided: should I shoot off after the others, or follow Maebh and find out what was going on? If I followed Maebh, the others might panic and get into trouble, so I made up my mind quickly. I shifted in mid-air into a peregrine falcon, for speed, and hurtled off after my friends. Unfortunately, because they were expecting a magpie, I almost gave them heart attacks because peregrine falcons are rather partial to smaller birds – for dinner!

They shot into a tree and cowered back against the trunk. I followed them, rapidly changing back to a magpie so that they wouldn't die of fright. 'Sorry, gang!' I said. 'I had to catch you up quickly. I forgot you'd be scared.'

'Oh, and isn't my heart pounding like the Great Bodhran of Brian Boru!' O'Liam groaned. 'Didn't I think my last hour had come entirely, so I did!'

I ignored him. 'Listen, T.A. The other magpie – it was Maebh!'

'Maebh? Are you sure?'

'Positive. I followed her. There was no magpie – just Maebh, running like a bat out of hell towards a castle back there. You stay here and wait for me. I'm going to go back and see what I can find out.'

'I think I'd rather come with you,' T.A. said.

'I don't think I would, at all,' O'Liam said miserably, 'but I don't want to be left all on my lonesome, neither.'

So the three of us retraced our wing-beats until we came to the castle. It wasn't much cop as castles go: it was in dire need of some repair. Walls were tumbling down, there were holes in the roof in which whole colonies of pigeons had made nests, and generally the whole place looked as if one good puff of wind would demolish it completely.

We perched on a nearby tree. 'You two wait here,' I ordered. T.A. opened her beak, but I held up a wing and shut her up. 'No, T.A. You stay here with O'Liam. If I'm not back in an hour, get home as fast as you can and tell Gwydion what's happened.'

'But –'

'Don't argue, T.A. Just do what I tell you for once, all right?'

She sighed, and settled back on her perch.

I dropped off the branch and up and over the castle wall. It was just as dilapidated inside as it was outside: great piles of rubbish lay everywhere, and as I watched somebody opened a shutter high up in the tower and emptied what looked suspiciously like a chamber-pot.

I thought about what would be the safest thing to change into: definitely not a mouse. I knew enough about castles to know that even the worst of them seemed to have large numbers of cats about, probably because the worst castles have rats and mice too! A large, very hairy dog was sleeping in the sunshine – an Irish wolfhound almost as big as a donkey. And as long as the dog stayed asleep, I'd be fine. I flew down into the shadowy doorway into the keep and shape-shifted into a wolf-hound. And immediately had to have a good scratch, because this particular hound didn't wear a flea-collar and didn't seem to have been bathed for years.

Then I went hunting. I stopped at the foot of a spiral stone stairway and listened. I could hear Maebh's bell-like voice and another, deeper voice, and I started up the stairway towards the sound.

The door of the chamber the voices were coming from was slightly ajar, and I stuck my nose in and gave it a shove. Then, happily disguised as the family pet, I went wagging into the room.

Maebh was there, sitting on a stool, but there was no one else in the room. So who had she been talking to?

And then a male voice, so close to me that I shot about two metres straight up in the air, spoke. 'Just because you saw a couple of magpies that didn't look right, Maebh, doesn't mean the Welsh witch is here. You aren't a real magpie yourself, so how would you know what a magpie acts like?'

'Oh, Master Henbane, I just know! I've never met a magpie that talked about the weather!'

All four of my legs gave way beneath me: I thought Henbane was gone for good. I'd vanished him right out of the Great Hall of Gwyddno Garanhir's palace in Cantre'r Gwaelod. I'd seen *all* of him disappear, every last little bit. Well, he still hadn't reappeared of course – but Henbane, unfortunately, was still around. And as far as I was concerned, the only thing worse than Henbane was an invisible Henbane.

Then matters got rapidly worse.

'Here, Mairead,' invisible Henbane cooed, 'come to Daddy!'

And I, apparently, was Mairead!

9

Well, what else could I do? I pootled over to where Master Henbane's voice was coming from thin air. Halfway there I remembered to wag my tail. An invisible hand descended on my head and scratched my ears. It felt quite nice, but I still wanted to bite him. Except I couldn't see anything to bite.

'Ah, Mairead, you're a fine beast, so you are, and you don't mind if you can't see me, do you?'

I wagged my tail again. Actually, I did mind. I would much rather be able to see my enemies, thank you very much. I wondered how soon I could politely remove myself from the pats and the doggy-woggy-itsy-bitsy talk. It was making me feel sick. And then I heard a low, thoroughly cheesed-off-sounding growl.

I looked behind me: coming through the chamber door was the real Mairead. Her hackles were standing up, her head was low and her teeth were bared. She was NOT wagging her tail. She walked towards me on stiff, angry legs, all the time snarling deep down in her massive chest. Her ears were flat to her narrow skull, and from the expression on her doggy face I didn't give much for my chances in a dog-fight.

Oops! I tried a tentative, hey-why-don't-you-and-me-be-friends? type wag. That didn't help. It only made her growl louder. She increased her speed and just as she gathered her haunches under her to spring on me, even though it would blow my cover completely, I thought it would be a good idea to make myself scarce. I shifted rapidly to a sparrow and shot out of the arrow-slit.

Behind me, there was utter silence. Even Mairead had stopped growling, completely mystified by where the rival dog – that had looked just like herself – had gone. I perched in the ivy outside the window and listened.

'Told you so!' I heard Maebh say, and then the sound of a hard slap.

'That will teach you respect to your elders and betters,' Henbane hissed.

'But I did tell you so!' Maebh wailed. 'I said the witch was here, and so she is. I know it's her!'

'She may be,' Henbane said. 'We knew that she would have to come back to keep her promise to Conor of the Land Beneath, or risk Ynys Haf dying of lack of rain. But she is no match for Conor, and certainly no match for me. I underestimated her last time. This time I shall win. I shall get rid of the Dragonking, and –'

'And I shall be Queen of Ynys Haf again!' Maebh crowed, and clapped her hands, apparently forgetting the slap.

'All we have to do is to wait until Conor has his revenge on the Witch, and then Ynys Haf is mine!'

'No, mine!' Maebh insisted. 'I'll be Queen. I shall, shan't I?'

Henbane didn't answer her: even if Maebh did wind up as Queen of Ynys Haf (which she would be doing over my dead body, I hasten to add!) then she would be a puppet-queen, and Henbane would be pulling the strings with his (invisible) hands. The thought was not a pleasant one.

I left the ivy and flew back to the tree where I'd left the others.

'Thank goodness you're back, Tanz,' T.A. squawked. 'I was beginning to get worried.'

I perched beside her. 'It's worse than I thought,' I said. 'It was Maebh all right, but Henbane's there as well.'

'But you vanished him!' T.A. protested. 'Aunty Fliss said she saw him disappear herself!'

'Oh, he disappeared all right,' I groaned. 'Now I've got an invisible enemy. Merlin was right.'

'It's my opinion that Lord Merlin usually is right, and most often correct as well,' O'Liam agreed. 'He has the most annoying habit of always being right, does he not, so?'

'Oh, he does,' I agreed. 'But last time he was behind everything that happened, and this time he isn't there setting me up.'

'No,' T.A. scratched her head with one claw, 'this time you're getting yourself out of the terrible pickle that Merlin's messing about landed you in.'

She was right, of course. And just like last time, Merlin was nowhere about. It was all up to me. I had no Nest to advise me, no Gwydion, no Flissy: just T.A., who was mainly mortal and to my mind shouldn't be here at all, and O'Liam of the Green Boots, who was a leprechaun, and subject to all the sneakiness that leprechauns, with the best will in the world, can't help. That isn't terribly good grammar, but I know what I mean.

'Come on. It doesn't matter that Henbane and Maebh are still part of the problem. We have to get to Conor and rescue Nest – yes, O'Liam, and Siobhan Flowerface too. I still think we should try to get Big Deirdre on our side.'

'Well, now, will you be needing me at all?' he asked. 'Because if you are not, and you are intending to talk to the giant, then there is a lot that I can be doing some very great distance away from here.'

'Of course we need you. But for the moment we'll forget about Big Deirdre. All right?'

'Oh, that makes me feel a lot better. "For the moment" indeed.'

Ahead we could see the sea: flat and blue, the sun glinting on small wavelets. Over the brow of the next hill was Big Deirdre's cottage, and part of me still wanted to go and try to talk the giantess into helping us. Getting close to her would be difficult, though, I knew that. After all, the Guardian of the Port could smell magic – and she'd certainly have no trouble detecting me, unless I could switch off my aura the way Nest showed me. The trouble was, I still wasn't terribly good at it.

So we flew away from the cottage, and headed for the Land Beneath. I'd worry about how we'd rescue Nest when we got there. Despite O'Liam moaning that he was so hungry he was dying of starvation, we didn't stop for food until we were quite close to the entrance to the Land Beneath, when it was almost evening and the sun was way down the sky, sitting on a patch of clouds and sploshing red all over the place.

We found a place in the hollow of a little hill, where there was a small cave that would shelter us.

'We'll stay here tonight,' I decided, 'and in the morning we'll decide how we're going to tackle Conor.'

O'Liam lay down and folded his hands on his stomach. 'I shall not be here when the sun comes up,

Lady. Sure, and my stomach is so empty it's having a long conversation with my backbone, so it is.'

'OK, O'Liam. I can take a hint as well as the next person. What's it to be? Pizza? Big Mac and fries? Fried chicken? What?'

'Yes, please,' he said.

'O'Liam, that is so piggish!' T.A. howled. 'But since you're asking, Tanz, me too!'

So we indulged ourselves, and ate junk food until we were so full we couldn't move away from the fire we'd built to crawl into the cave. Well, we could, but it was a fine, warm night and the stars were so big and bright they looked as if we could reach out and touch them. So I magicked some sleeping bags – naturally, a green one for O'Liam this time again – and we crawled in and settled down beside the fire.

It must have been almost dawn, because there was an apricot glow in the eastern sky when I woke, although at first I kept my eyes tightly shut. I had this really weird sensation of whizzing through the air. It made me feel a bit sick. I put it down to over-indulging on the Big Macs. And then I heard T.A. shriek and opened my eyes.

I WAS whizzing through the air!

Big Deirdre had scooped us up, sleeping bags and all. I struggled to get awake enough to shift us all into something – anything – that would get us out of there. But it was too late. Big Deirdre shoved me and T.A. inside a cage and clanged the door shut. No problem, for a witch, you might think? Wrong. The cage was made entirely of iron bars. It wiped out my magic altogether.

Then I began to hope: O'Liam could deal with iron. He'd get us out. But Big Deirdre obviously knew that O'Liam was the Ironfinder: his cage was made of strong, thick leather.

So there we were, trapped.

The giantess lifted the cage to eye level and peered at us. 'Big Deirdre could smell you, witch, as soon as you were in a ten mile distance, she could. And now she's got you altogether and entirely. And that's only in the hand that's to the right of me! In my other hand – well, if it isn't a nasty, sneaky, treacherous little leprechaun. One of them nasty wee beasties that killed my poor little innocent babby and hung his handsome little head on the wall. Ooh, leprechaun! I'm going to enjoy killing you!'

O'Liam curled up on the floor of his leather cage and moaned, softly. I wished there was something I could do to help, but I felt so sick and miserable and weak. The iron was all around me, sapping my strength.

Big Deirdre carried us back to her cottage, and before she shifted back to her smaller size, she opened the front door and shoved the two cages in. I'd hoped she might put us side by side, but she was too canny for that: she put O'Liam on one side of the room, and T.A. and me on the other. Then she shifted and came in after us, shutting the door firmly behind her. She stood in front of the iron cage, her hands on her hips.

'Pooh!' she said disgustedly, 'your magic stinks, witch. I shall get rid of you very quick. You make my house smell.'

Coming from her that was rich. I doubt if she'd had

a bath since Christmas – and I don't even want to think which year!

T.A. was losing her temper. 'What do you mean, get rid of us?' she demanded. 'You wouldn't dare kill us – my friend's the Dragonqueen of Ynys Haf! The Dragonking will be seriously upset if you kill her – or me!' she added hastily.

'Shut up, T.A.!' I muttered. 'Don't dare her, for goodness sake!'

'Oooh, I wouldn't dare, eh? Well, miss, you're entirely wrong about that. I'd kill you like that!' – and the giantess snapped her fingers – 'if I'd a mind to, I would. And your Dragonqueen as well. I'd probably step on the Dragonking if he were foolish enough to try to come here, so there! Oh, if I wanted to, I'd kill you quick as I'd kill a rat. But I've got a better plan. I'm going to use you as bait!'

'Bait?' T.A. and I said together.

'Like little wiggly wee maggots on a fishing line. Only I'm not after fish, no I'm not. I'm after that wee devil Conor. And he is after you, is he not? So if I dangle you before his nasty little nose, I'll have the lot of you. And THEN I'll kill you!' She put her head on one side. 'Now, just behave yourselves and don't be interrupting me at all. Haven't I a friend coming for tea and here's me with nothing to eat in the house?'

It seemed kind of weird that our captor was planning a tea party! However, as soon as she'd picked up her basket and left the cottage, I called out to O'Liam, who was still curled up in a ball on the floor of his thick leather cage.

'O'Liam, are you all right?'

'As all right as a dead leprechaun is likely to be, to be sure,' he whimpered.

'Oh, come on, O'Liam. You aren't dead yet! Where there's life, there's hope!' T.A. said firmly.

'I might as well be dead,' the little man replied. 'For whatever Big Deirdre has in store for me, it will not be a pleasant whatever, no, not at all.'

'O'Liam, if you could only talk to the iron of our cage and convince it to let us out,' I suggested, 'then we could let you out of your cage and we could all get out of here.'

'Oh, it's a wonderful idea entirely, Lady,' O'Liam agreed, still curled in his ball. 'But that iron has been through the very hot fire and is altogether above itself. I could only get control of that if I could touch it. And with you over here and me over there, here we shall be until we die, because my arms are of a shortness that only reaches nearly to my knees. No, I'm going to die,' he moaned. 'You at least have a wee chance to get away. Since she has already said she is intending to put you on her fishing line, so to speak. No, you might just as well say goodbye to me now.'

And that, it seemed, was that. We were finished before we'd even started.

10

The iron floor of the cage was not comfortable to sit on, despite the sleeping bags that Big Deirdre had chucked in with us. After half an hour my rear end felt as if it would never be the same again. T.A. and I leaned back-to-back.

'Another fine mess you've got me into, Stanley!' T.A. said after a while. Good old T.A.: she can make jokes even when a giantess is about to use you as a maggot!

'You were the one who insisted on coming,' I said. 'Don't blame me.'

'I told you, it was the Ant who made me come,' she said, digging me in the ribs with her elbow. 'She foresaw some trouble I could get you out of.'

'Looks like she scryed wrong this time, then, didn't she?' Except that Aunt Ant was rarely wrong. Well, there's a first time for everything. 'Oh, T.A., I feel awful. The iron is really getting to me. My legs are wobbly and my head aches. It feels like I've got 'flu or something.'

T.A. grabbed her hair with both hands and tugged. 'What can we do? O'Liam's no help – even if his cage was closer I doubt if he could pull himself together enough to do anything. He's so scared. I wish I could give him a cuddle.'

T.A.'s a bit like my Mam – she thinks a cuddle cures everything, too!

'I don't suppose Gwydion – ?' T.A. went on.

'He isn't fit enough yet. He won't get here for ages.

Probably won't see him at all, ever again, under the circumstances. Either Big Deirdre or Conor will have done something terrible to us before Gwydion even thinks about coming.'

'Well, looking on the bright side, even if we had reached Conor, what does he want? Me, for a start. O'Liam, for seconds, and Maebh. Two you wouldn't let him have – at least, I hope not, Tanz! – and the third you can't.'

'Who says I can't?'

'What? You mean you'd calmly hand over that poor, idiotic, half-witted female to Conor? And take away her magic into the bargain?'

I sighed. 'I s'pose not. The awful thing is that even though I can't see myself handing over Maebh, Conor won't be satisfied with anything else. There's an awful problem with being a good witch, T.A. I've got a worse conscience than Jiminy Cricket.'

She swivelled round and gave me a hug. 'Wouldn't have you any other way, Tanz.'

Then Big Deirdre came back, laden with all sorts of goodies: fish straight out of the sea, a very large piece of ham, apples and all sorts of other stuff. Then she made soda bread and a cake that had treacle in it and smelled wonderful. Even O'Liam sat up. The smell of food made me feel worse – the iron had even affected my appetite. But T.A.'s mouth watered even though she was shut up in a cage awaiting her last hour! She didn't get any, of course. Big Deirdre obviously wasn't going to the expense of feeding her prisoners.

Half-way through the afternoon, someone knocked on the door.

'Is there anyone at home inside at all at all?' a voice said. It was a girly, fluttery, breathy little voice. 'Is there someone kind inside who is expecting a good friend for a tasty tea, so?'

'Oh there is, there is.' Big Deirdre took off her enormous pinny and hung it on a hook, Then she patted her hair and opened both halves of the stable door. 'Will you come in, old friend, and welcome.'

'I'm entirely honoured to do so, indeed and for certain, Deirdre dear.'

I don't know what I was expecting, but it certainly wasn't what had arrived. It was a she – I think – but despite the little-girly voice, she was almost as big as Deirdre. She had a curious greenish glow about her, her hair was long, wild and matted as a bird's nest, she was wearing a floaty greenish dress that seemed to have a life of its own, the way it drifted about her person, she wore horizontally striped green and yellow stockings, and what looked remarkably like hob-nailed boots on her feet. She also had a wart on her nose, a tooth missing in front, so that her girly voice had a whistle and a splutter to it, and her eyes both looked in different directions at once. She made Big Deirdre look like a glamour model!

I nudged T.A. 'Get a load of that, T.A.!' I whispered.

'I'm looking!' she said, and hid a giggle in a snort.

'No talking, maggots!' Big Deirdre thundered.

'Oh, and what might you have in that big old cage, Deirdre?' the visitor trilled.

'A nasty pair of witches,' the giantess replied. 'What I caught sneaking into our country in an entirely shady and unsatisfactory, sneaky and wholly illegal style of way.'

'Ugh!' the visitor replied. 'Witches! What will you do with them?'

'Oh, I have plans for them, Cornelia, I do so. But the plans don't include them staying alive at all!'

The two friends chortled happily.

Then the visitor spotted the other cage. 'And what's this wee balled-up creature over here, may I ask, if I'm not being entirely too curious, Deirdre dear?'

O'Liam curled himself up tighter.

'It is a leprechaun. And you know what I do to leprechauns.'

The visitor was peering through the leather bars of O'Liam's cage. 'The back of its neck looks strangely familiar, Deirdre. What like is it, this leprechaun?'

'Well, would you believe it or not, Cornelia, but haven't I only gone and captured O'Liam of the Green Boots!'

Now I was watching big ugly Cornelia, and I swear she staggered back. She gasped and her hands flew to her face. 'O'Liam? You've caught the O'Liam? Of the Green Boots? O'Liam Ironfinder?'

'I have, so. The very same person. Sit yourself up, you wee vermin, and pay attention when you're being discussed!' Deirdre bellowed, and poked O'Liam through the bars with a stick. Reluctantly, he sat up, but he didn't look at her or the visitor.

'Oh, is it yourself, Cornelia?' he muttered. 'How might you be doing these days?'

'I'm as you see me, O'Liam,' Cornelia replied

tartly. 'Fit and fine and rearing to go. But yourself is in a fine state, are you not?'

'Oh, I am so.'

'Oh, leave the wee ratty creature,' Deirdre ordered. 'Come away and have a nice drink and a bit of tea, Cornelia. Tell me all the gossip!'

Oh, boy, could they gossip? They went on like a mothers' meeting. They ran down just about everyone in the neighbourhood, pulled apart their reputations, their looks, their life-styles and their personal habits. It was dark when Cornelia finally left. The giantess hugged her on the doorstep. 'Don't be a stranger, now!' she commanded.

'Thank you for my good tea,' Cornelia replied dutifully, 'will you come and do me the favour of taking tea with me next week?'

'Oh, I will indeed,' Deirdre agreed, beaming. 'And a fine honour it will be!'

Good. If she had something to look forward to, maybe she'd be in a reasonable temper. Not that I imagined she'd be in a good enough temper to let us go, but she might not dispose of O'Liam until the morning. She didn't.

'I'll let you live, just for tonight,' she said, poking him through the bars of his cage. 'But in case you are thinking I am being kindly at all, I am letting you live just so you can stay awake all night and think about how I'm going to kill you. And I shall go to sleep and dream about doing it. And when I've finished dreaming about that, I shall dream about killing Conor of the Land Beneath.'

She clambered up the wooden ladder to her bedroom, and we heard the thump, thump of her moving about. Then she settled down, there was silence for a short while, and then – she began to snore. To say that she would have woken the dead was an understatement. She wouldn't only have woken them, she'd have made them put their dead fingers in their dead ears, as well!

'O'Liam?' I whispered loudly. 'Are you awake?'

'Of course I'm awake. Doesn't my stomach think my throat's forgotten what food is? And a person who is about to die at any minute finds it entirely impossible to sleep,' the leprechaun said bitterly. 'And haven't things just got even worser?'

'What?' I said in alarm. 'What do you mean they've got worser?'

'Deirdre's visitor.'

'What about her?' T.A. was taking notice now.

'I know her of old, Lady. Cornelia is the one and only Bog Fairy. She's a terrible creature, so, but – well, we have what you might call a bit of a history.'

'A bit of a – what do you mean, O'Liam?'

'Ah, we met one day – when I was a giddy young leprechaun, you understand, barely a hundred and seventy, with not a whole lot of sense in my head. And didn't me and the Bog Fairy dally for a wee little while beside a stream, and ever since, the Bog Fairy's decided she's in love with me. Mind,' he added hastily, 'she was entirely better-looking in those days.'

Personally, I doubted it. 'The Bog Fairy's in love with you?'

'Aye. And extremely embarrassing it is too as well,

to be sure,' the little man moaned. 'Didn't she go straight off and tell the whole world we were about to jump the broomstick and put our shoes under the same bed? As if I'd think of marrying the likes of her when there's Siobhan Flowerface about! Ah, Siobhan, Siobhan,' he sighed.

'You Casanova!' T.A. said. 'You devil, O'Liam! Romancing the poor little Bog Fairy and then dumping her!' And she fell about laughing, so loud I thought Big Deirdre might hear her and wake up.

'It isn't funny in the slightest,' O'Liam said with wounded dignity. 'But it won't make the least little bit of difference. I'll still be dead as soon as Big Deirdre wakes up.'

He had a point. But for once, O'Liam was wrong.

T.A. and I were sitting uncomfortably back-to-back in the cage, and I was beginning to feel so ill that I thought I might die long before Big Deirdre used us as bait. I had started to shiver, and felt feverish and sick, which is what iron does to me. And then T.A. nudged me.

'Listen!'

'What?'

'There's somebody at the door!'

'Who?'

'Well how should I know? I can't see through wood, stupid!'

The door opened, slowly, silently, and a large shape tiptoed into the room. Well, I say tiptoed. It's hard to tiptoe in hob-nail boots.

'It's the Bog Fairy!' T.A' breathed.

We watched as Cornelia tiptoed across the room. She'd changed her dress for an even floatier one, a short one that didn't hide the muscular calves under the stripey stockings, and she'd put a matching bow in her wild hair.

She reached O'Liam's leather cage and bent down. 'O'Liam, you dear thing, are you awake at all?'

'No!' O'Liam muttered. 'Will you go away, Bog Fairy?'

'I've come to let you out,' the Bog Fairy whispered loudly. 'I'm going to rescue you, O'Liam, so that Big Deirdre can't kill you at all, and then I shall take you back to my cosy wee bog and we shall jump the broomstick together and put our shoes side by side. Oh, I can picture it fine,' she cooed, clasping her large, rather hairy hands. 'Your wee green boots next to my wee hobnails!'

Wee hobnails? She had to be joking. O'Liam could have lived in those boots they were so big!

'If you don't mind, I'd rather stay here and die,' O'Liam muttered.

'Oh, you're teasing, you naughty wee thing,' the Bog Fairy chortled girlishly, and bent to the leather lock on the leather cage.

'Big Deirdre,' O'Liam shrieked, 'come quick, I'm being stolen!'

Upstairs, the snoring ceased, and there was silence for a few seconds. Then came the sound of a heavy body turning over, and the snoring began again.

'Shut up, O'Liam,' I hissed. 'Of course you must let the Bog Fairy rescue you! Think about all the advantages!' The advantages I meant, of course, was that once O'Liam was out of his cage, he could get the big key from the hook on the wall and let us out of ours!

'Advantages, Lady? What advantages are there in marriage to a Bog Fairy? A bog is an awful, terrible place to live, and with anyone else there might be compensations, but –'

'Shut up, O'Liam,' T.A. and I said together. 'He doesn't mean it, Bog Fairy!' I said. 'He's just playing hard to get!'

'Oh, I know that, witches!' she chortled. 'He's a dear wee fellow with a grand sense of humour.' She stopped bothering with the leather strap and ripped it off the cage. T.A. and I winced. Then she reached in, and dragged O'Liam out by the ankle from where he was cowering in the corner.

'Right,' I called. 'O'Liam, get the –'

It was too late. O'Liam had been tucked under the Bog Fairy's sweaty armpit, and was disappearing out the door.

11

I slithered to the floor of the cage and put my head in my hands. 'That's done it,' I groaned. 'O'Liam's gone, and when Big Deirdre wakes up she's not going to be a happy teddy. She'll probably take it out on us.'

T.A. prodded me in the ribs. 'Oh, come on, Tanz. Look on the bright side! We're still alive, aren't we, and you know what I always say –'

'If you're going to say "where there's life there's hope," T.A,' I said crossly, 'or sing "Always look on the bright side of life", then please don't. Because right now, I feel so ill that even if the entire Swansea police force made a dawn raid on Big Deirdre, I couldn't even raise a cheer.'

Well, there weren't any big, tough constables, but there was one very small, very frightened leprechaun.

He crept in to Big Deirdre's cottage about two hours after the Bog Fairy had carried him off to her love-nest. He lifted the latch on the door and tottered in, shaking from head to foot and soaking wet.

'O'Liam!' T.A. whispered, 'You came back!'

'Well of course I did. Wouldn't I rather be shut up in a cage and killed entirely than stay one minute longer with Herself? Ooh, she's a frightening creature, that one, and me in fear of my life the entire time.'

'How did you get away?' T.A. wanted to know.

'Never mind how he got away,' I croaked. 'O'Liam, let us out, quick.'

O'Liam tottered across to our cage, pulled himself upright, folded his arms and said sternly to the cage, 'Now look, iron –'

'Never mind talking to it, O'Liam!' I shrieked as quietly as I could, 'Get the damn key!'

'Patience!' the leprechaun sniffed, but got a stool, climbed up and reached down the iron key to our cage. In a flash the padlock was off, and T.A. half-carried me out of the deadly iron cage that was sapping my strength. I was so weak I could hardly walk.

I had to get right away from its influence as quickly as I could. While I was close enough to see it, I was close enough for it to affect me. 'Let's get out of here,' I said.

We began to tiptoe across the floor towards the door, and in seconds were outside, me first, O'Liam next, and T.A. last. I took a deep, deep, very relieved sort of breath, and began to feel better instantly. The strength began to come back into my arms and legs and my headache receded into a small ache at the back of my skull.

It was a beautiful day: a slight sea-mist veiled the rising sun, and it gave the peachy light a pearly, translucent look. I looked about me, feeling glad to be alive, and free, and –

And then T.A. slammed the door behind her and we all three of us froze. I looked over my shoulder at the cottage. A large, sleepy face peered suspiciously out of an upstairs window.

'Quick!' I yelled. 'Run!'

So I shifted us into blue hares (it took a little longer than usual because my magic had been drained like a car battery by the iron cage) and we stretched our legs and – literally – hared off. Although we were smaller than the brown hares I was more used to in Wales, the blue hare was the only one that lived in Ireland, so we were stuck with it. Not that I minded: it was small, fast, and dedicated to staying out of trouble. By the time Big Deirdre had thundered down her stairs, shifted into giant size and set off in long-legged pursuit, we were out of there, whisking up a mountain, springing from boulder to boulder until we came to a small hollow where we could shift back, hide and rest. Oh, and eat. Now that I was away from the iron my appetite had come back with a vengeance.

We had bacon, eggs, grilled tomatoes, fried bread, mushrooms, bread-and-butter and big mugs of tea. Oh, and I had HP sauce and O'Liam discovered tomato ketchup. He soon had a big red ring of it round his mouth and an expression of bliss on his little golden face.

Once we had eaten, T.A. couldn't resist it. 'So, what happened with the Bog Fairy, O'Liam?'

He sat up straight and put on an expression of offended dignity. 'That is for me to know, T.A.,' he said firmly, 'and I will not be countenancing the discussing of it. Not ever. If I even begin to think about it I shall be riding the night mare for the rest of my natural life, I shall, and a terrible ride it would be, to be sure.' He shuddered, and hunched his head down into his shoulders protectively. 'I might even break out in spots at the memory, so I might!'

'Oh, go on, give us a hint,' T.A. teased. 'How did you manage to get away?'

He shuddered. 'This I will tell you, and no more. After a long, long and terrible journey through moorland and bog – especially bog – we came to the place where she lives, which is also in the thick of a bog and not where a normal person would live from choice, but isn't she the Bog Fairy and different from the normal style of folks?'

'And?' prompted T.A.

'Well, she wept and said that I had forsaken her, and I said that I had not. We to-ed and fro-ed for a while and a bit, but after a time didn't she sit right up, bold as you like, and ask me for a kiss. A kiss! Would you try to believe that, if you can? What like sort of person goes about asking other persons for kisses? But I have a certain natural intelligence and a certain, even if I say it myself, craftiness –'

'You can say that again!' I muttered, so he did.

'Then,' O'Liam went on, 'I said that I would, indeed, give her a kiss. But first, I said, she must close her lovely eyes tight as a new mushroom and pooch out her ruby-red lips like so.' He screwed up his eyes and stuck out his lips.

'And then what did you do?'

'Oh, Lady,' he replied, 'I did exactly what any other leprechaun in his rightsome mind would have done. I ran. I ran so fast I am amazed she didn't feel the wind of my passing like the mighty gale that is in the trees on a stormy night. I put such distance between myself and the Bog Fairy so fast, that before she even opened her eyes – and doesn't each one of them look in an entirely different direction – wasn't I half a mile gone and still going?'

T.A. snorted. 'Good thinking, O'Liam. And thanks for rescuing us.'

'I second that.' I patted the leprechaun's shoulder. 'We really, really owe –'

'I've told you before, Lady,' O'Liam shrieked, covering his ears with both hands, 'don't say such things to me. It isn't wise at all.'

'But O'Liam, if we can't trust you by now, who can we trust?'

'I'll say it again, Lady. Leprechauns do not change their spots, and sneakiness is in our blood. It amazes me sometimes that I can walk in a straight line at all when my brain is forever telling me to be crooked, so it is.'

I shrugged. 'Well, O'Liam, if you say so. But we really are grateful.'

'Grateful is fine. Grateful is good. But do not ever be owing me anything, for it is in my nature to take what is owed.'

Personally I couldn't believe that the little man would ever double-cross us after all we had been through together. No, whether he knew it or not, I was certain he was entirely on our side.

'Right,' T.A. said when we'd cleared away the remnants of our meal. 'What are we going to do next?'

I'd been hoping she wouldn't ask that, because I didn't have a clue. 'Um,' I said.

'Well,' T.A. rattled on, not waiting for more of a reply (which was just as well, because I didn't actually have one), 'let's discuss exactly what we've got to cope with, shall we?'

Sounded like a good idea to me. Perhaps by the time we'd finished talking about that, something useful would have occurred to me.

'Well, first,' she said, bossily, 'why are we here?'

'Good question,' O'Liam and I said together.

She glared at us. 'Well, because Conor of the Land Beneath seems to think you owe him a lot of stuff, right?'

'Stuff?' O'Liam spluttered, 'I am not "stuff". I am O'Liam Ironfinder, not "stuff"!'

'Sorry, O'Liam,' T.A. said, but she was off again. 'Come on, Tanz, you list what you've got to do.'

'Well, Conor is mad at me because he says I stole O'Liam – which I did, I suppose, except that O'Liam is a human being and no one can own a –'

'Will the pair of you give over insulting me?' O'Liam was dark, purplish gold with fury, 'I am not a human being, no, not at all I am not, not the leastest little bit!'

My turn to apologise. 'Sorry, O'Liam, that was just a slip of the tongue.'

'Hmmph.'

'No one can own anyone else, whatever they are. All right O'Liam?'

'All right. And wasn't I saying the exact same thing to the Bog Fairy not half a day back?'

'What else, Tanz?' T.A. said impatiently.

'Conor wants Maebh – but Maebh without her magic.'

'She hasn't got much to begin with.'

'About as much magic as she has brain,' I said. 'But all the same, I don't feel I can let Conor have either of his two requests. Although I might be able to come to terms with giving him Henbane. If I could see him,' I added glumly. 'Then, of course, there's what we want from Conor. We want Nest back, unharmed, and O'Liam wants his Siobhan Flowerface, right O'Liam?'

'Oh, I do so. And a visit to my Mammy if it can be fitted in.'

'I can't work out how come Conor still has Nest,' T.A. said. 'He shouldn't be able to keep her, she's just as magic as he is, isn't she?'

'Well, she is. But maybe it's a different sort of magic, and that's how he's doing it.'

'So, what are we going to do?' T.A. pushed.

'Try to be just as sneaky as the average leprechaun, for which we shall need O'Liam's help.'

The leprechaun sat up straight and paid attention. He also looked worried.

'O'Liam, could we get into the Land Beneath without Conor realising we are there?'

The little man screwed up his sharp, golden face. 'If we were exceedingly small, we could most certainly, Lady. You could bewhizzle us into some style of tiny creature and in we should go. But what can tiny creatures do against Conor of the Land Beneath?'

'They can get inside, and then change, that's what.'

'But then he would see us,' O'Liam pointed out.

'That's a problem, true. But I think we'll get inside first, and worry about that afterwards. The trouble is, that if I take Nest away without his permission, and I manage somehow to get Siobhan Flowerface out without his permission, and I don't give him Maebh or O'Liam, he's going to be seriously rattier than he is at the moment. It's a terrible problem.'

'There must be a way round it. I've been thinking, Tanz –'

'Careful!' I warned, 'You don't do it very often. Don't strain your brain.'

'Ha, ha, Tanz. Shut up and listen, will you?'

'Sorry.'

'There's one other thing Conor might possibly want.'

'What?'

'Me.'

I stared at her. 'And your point is?'

'Well, you could use me as bait, right?'

'What good would that do?'

'Well, I could sort of distract him, while you got away with Nest and O'Liam's girlfriend.'

'And then who rescues you? No, T.A. I was thinking more of leaving you out of this altogether, after the last time you got involved with Conor.'

'No way!' T.A.'s face was indignant. 'I'm not staying outside like an optional extra while you two take all the risks! No, we all go together. Or else.'

'Or else what?'

'I'll think of something, trust me.'

And she probably would. Which was why all three of us ended up, the next day, paying a visit to Conor, Lord of the Land Beneath…

12

We travelled throughout the rest of the day, not stopping until we were very close to where Conor of the Land Beneath had the entrance to his underground kingdom, and then we found a place to sleep inside a small cave half-way up a mountain. We weren't disturbed by any giants, Bog Fairies or anything else that night, but I hardly slept a wink anyway. The thing was, I wasn't looking forward AT ALL to invading Conor's court a second time – especially now I knew how very dangerous he could be. If you know anything about me at all, you will know two things: (a) I'm a serious coward, and (b) I don't like having to hang about waiting to prove it!

Birdsong woke the others early, just as the sun came up, and once we had eaten (O'Liam had tomato sauce on toast, would you believe?) I got ready to shift us all into birds – bullfinches, for a change, I thought. And then I got the feeling that we were being watched.

Slowly, I swivelled my head round. I was right. A few metres higher up the mountain, on a bare, rocky outcrop, a man was sitting. He wore a brownish, very tatty robe, and sat with both hands outstretched and cupped before him, as if he was holding something.

'O'Liam,' I whispered, 'who's that?'

O'Liam turned round, looked up, and beamed. 'Oh, well, if it isn't Brother Kevin!' he said delightedly. 'Will you look at the state of the man, so. He's been out in all weathers since I don't know when. Hello there, your holiness!' O'Liam called. 'Have they not hatched yet?'

The man shook his head, gravely.

'Haven't what hatched, O'Liam?' I asked.

'The eggs.'

'Eggs?'

'Blackbird eggs. Sure, and wasn't the kind feller sitting there minding his own business when the mammy bird came along. So still he was sitting that she went and laid her eggs right in the palm of his hand, so.'

'She laid her eggs in his hand?'

'Didn't I just say so? And hasn't the good thing been sitting there like a statue ever since, waiting for them to hatch! Are you all right, Brother Kevin dear?'

The man's voice was creaky, as if he didn't use it very often. 'Oh, I am so. But I thank you most kindly for taking the trouble to ask.'

'Can we be doing anything for you before we make ourselves to be not here at all, Brother Kevin?'

'Oh, you can so.'

'Just speak the words, Kevin, and it shall be done.'

'Would you be so good as to get me some water? I've a powerful thirst on me, and I've had nothing to drink for the past six weeks.'

'Six weeks?' I said. 'He ought to be dead!'

'And he would be so if it were not for the fact that he is entirely holy,' O'Liam said reprovingly. 'Now, Lady, will you get yourself up there and give the feller a drink when he asks?'

I clambered obediently up the rocks, magicked a bottle of ice-cold mineral water and a straw and held it for Brother Kevin to suck. It disappeared like rainwater down a drain and he closed his eyes and sighed with pleasure.

'Are you hungry?' I asked.

'I am so, Lady,' the man replied. He had tired, kindly blue eyes, and his face was brown and wrinkled from the sun and framed by white hair like a dandelion clock.

I produced a ham sandwich and fed it to him. When it was gone he closed his eyes and smiled ecstatically. Then he opened them and twinkled his eyes at me, as if he had a great big secret.

'Would you like to see my eggs?' he asked, and removed his right hand, which was cupped over the eggs in his palm. The eggs, which lay in a nest of dried grass, were pale bluey-green with brown splashes, and as I gazed at them a harrassed looking brown bird flew to his shoulder and perched.

'Ah, it's the Mammy. Hello, Mammy!' he said, and the bird cheeped a reply.

'They're beautiful!' I said solemnly. 'When do you think they will hatch?'

He sighed. 'Any day now, I hope. I've been sitting here a powerful long time, and the bottom on me is quite numb. Would you do one more thing for me before you go?'

I nodded.

'Would you scratch my back, just a wee bit? Sure and I've had such an itch for the past fortnight and can't be getting at it at all.'

I obliged, and scratched hard through the rough robe, setting clouds of dust flying. O'Liam and T.A. joined us, and both peered at the eggs.

'Oh, that was lovely, so it was,' Brother Kevin said. 'Now, Lady, if I can do anything at all for you once my eggs hatch, you can be sure I shall be doing it as prompt as I can.'

O'Liam had his ears down to the eggs, listening. 'And that will not be long, Brother Kevin,' he said. 'Didn't I just hear the tap, tap of the wee things on the inside of the shell?'

Brother Kevin smiled. 'Oh, to be sure that's a good thing. Then, as soon as the babies have all growed up and flown away, I can be about my business.'

'He's going to wait for the fledglings to fly?' I whispered as we walked away.

'He is, so,' O'Liam confirmed. 'The man's a saint entirely.'

We said our goodbyes to Brother Kevin, and at the foot of the hill I shifted us into bullfinches. We spread our black/white/grey wings and lifted our rosy bodies off the hillside and into the air, winging towards Conor's Land. Needless to say my bullfinch brain was going quietly berserk trying to come up with a plan for once we were inside. I hoped we wouldn't come face to face with Conor before I thought of something!

O'Liam led the way to a clearing in a small wood, his white bullfinch rump flashing like morse code ahead of us. He perched in a tree and waited.

'There's the way in,' he chirped, 'and I can tell you that the nerves in my body is all standing on end and jangling, Lady.'

'It'll be OK,' T.A. assured him. 'Tanz will take care of us.'

I wished I felt as certain of that as she did! Still, it was up to me, right? 'O'Liam, which would be less likely to be noticed in the Land Beneath, spiders or ants?'

'Oh, ants, Lady. Spiders are killed on sight, for Conor will not put up with their webs in his palace. They give him the shivers, for he once met a lady that could shift at will into a great big huge spider, and he's never forgotten her. She caught him in her web and he would have died, except Maebh freed him.'

'Merch Corryn Du!' T.A. breathed, and I nodded. It couldn't be anyone else.

'Let me get this straight,' I said. '*Maebh* freed him from the Spiderwitch – and he still wants her delivered to him without her magic, right? Despite the fact that she probably saved his life?'

'Oh, he does, so!' O'Liam confirmed. 'For after she freed him she would not have him for her husband. He was only a leprechaun lord she said, and she would be a Queen one day. He was mortally offended by her saying so. He is king in all but name.'

'So even though Maebh once saved his life, he still wants revenge?'

O'Liam nodded.

'He's not nice, is he?' T.A. commented.

'Not at all. And he's sneaky, too, T.A. Just remember that and we might get out of this alive.'

I changed us into large wood ants, which wouldn't be unusual on the dried leaves on the floor of the wood, and we scuttled towards the opening in the hollow tree that was the way to the Land Beneath.

There was a door but it had a big enough gap beneath it to allow the three of us to creep through quite easily.

O'Liam led the way: his shiny little black legs flashed as he scurried down and down into the earth. We passed one or two leprechauns on their way up, and flattened ourselves against the earth of the walls so that we shouldn't be seen. But then we were in the Great Hall of the Land Beneath, and there was Conor. He was seated at the large conference table surrounded by his advisers and the little man with the long beard and even longer quill pen who did his writing for him. It was beneath Conor's dignity to learn to read or write himself when he had servants to do it for him. He was, after all, Lord of the Land Beneath and King of All Leprechauns.

Which was all very well, I thought, but I am the Lady, Dragonqueen of Ynys Haf, and I am blowed if I am going to be bullied by a four-foot bloke with big eyes and golden skin and a sneaky reputation.

Conor was speaking. 'I don't care,' he said softly to the underling who had obviously said something, because he was standing beside Conor's chair, cringing. 'I don't care at all if the half-fairy is fading away entirely. If she dies, she dies. She will not leave the Land Beneath until I say so. And I shall not say so, no, not at all, until I have the Lady of Ynys Haf and her friend Haf, and Maebh, and the traitor O'Liam, all within my power. And then we shall see who is the greatest!'

'But what if the half-fairy dies, your Greatness?' grovelled the underling, a short (even for a leprechaun, I mean) round person with tufts of grey hair sticking out like grass on his otherwise bald head.

'Then she dies, Feargal Shamrock!' Conor hissed.

'And the Lady of Ynys Haf will be none the wiser when she comes to bargain for her life.'

'That's what you think!' I thought fiercely. But it sounded as if Nest was in real trouble, and I now knew what the first thing was that I had to do. Find Nest and help her. Fast. See? I said something would occur to me in time, didn't I?

'So I'll thank you, Feargal Shamrock,' Conor said smoothly, 'to get out of my sight and go and do your duty. Look after the prisoner and try to make sure that she doesn't die. Because if she does, I promise that you will die also.'

Feargal Shamrock gulped. The Adam's apple slid up and down in his throat and perspiration popped out on his pale – his very pale – golden face.

'Ah, I hear what you say, your Greatness,' he replied, and, spinning round he set off at a great whack for the nearest exit.

'Come on, quick,' I whispered, and the three of us set off, sprinting at the heels of the unhappy Feargal.

'Ha!' O'Liam puffed behind me, 'sure and isn't it time that one got his comeuppance! Always lording it over me, he was so! Just because I was an Ironfinder and he was the Seeker of the Sacred Shamrock! Above himself entirely, for doesn't the stuff grow like a weed all over Erin! Sure, and aren't there whole fields of it, green as grass and twice as thick. But iron, ah, now iron is a different sort of fish entirely, and –'

'Shut up, O'Liam. He's getting away,' I panted.

O'Liam shut up, and we pelted as fast as we could after Feargal Shamrock before he disappeared around the bends in the twisting corridors.

13

Feargal Shamrock scuttled down the corridor with three galloping ants on his heels. He opened a door at the end of it, and we followed him down a flight of stairs, through another door and down a long, spiralling tunnel.

A sick feeling came into my stomach: no wonder Nest was dying if she was being kept so far from sunlight and air. The *Tylwyth Teg* are above-ground creatures, and for her to be shut away in the depths of the earth must be terrible for her.

We went down so far into the earth that I wondered if soon we'd hit the boiling volcanic magma at the earth's core. OK, so I'm exaggerating, but it felt that way. The deeper we went, the dimmer the light was, and by the time we reached the heavy wooden door of Nest's prison, it was as gloomy as the inside of a cinema when the lights go off before the film starts.

I said it was a 'wooden door', and I suppose it was, sort of. But it was made not of planks but of black, snaky tree-roots, twined and woven and twisted and plaited until it was twice as impenetrable and ten times as tough as an ordinary wooden door. It was sealed with a great wooden bar dropped across it and locked with a hasp and an iron-hard wooden padlock. Feargal unhooked a huge key from his belt and unlocked the padlock, puffed and panted as he strained to lift the heavy bar from across the slots on each side of the door, and finally pulled the door open.

Inside, the air was hot and dark, with only a faint

light from the tunnel filtering in. At first I couldn't see Nest at all, and then I saw her: chained to the wall with iron chains. I cowered down behind a loose piece of gravel so that the iron couldn't get to me – the last thing I wanted was that I should get the iron-sickness too.

Nest lay slumped against the wall, her eyes half-closed. She was limp as a pile of wet washing and I kept peeping over my bit of gravel, scared that she might have died already, and that we would have been too late. I knew what it was like to have iron around me: I had only been in the cage overnight, and Nest had been shut away for days and days – maybe weeks.

Feargal Shamrock bent over her and prodded her. 'Wake up, fairy,' he shouted in her ear. 'You aren't allowed to die. Conor says yous must stay alive. Will you open your eyes when I tell you? Are you entirely dead already, so?'

I was horribly afraid. For a long while Nest didn't move, and then she stirred sluggishly and opened her eyes.

Her voice was creaky and hoarse. 'No, I'm not dead. I'm not going to die. When my nephew Gwydion Dragonking comes, Conor of the Land Beneath will be sorry. Gwydion will punish him.'

'Will you eat a bit of bread and cheese if I bring it to you?' Feargal asked anxiously. 'It's a whole week of seven days since you ate more than a wee crumb, so it is.'

'I can't eat,' Nest croaked. 'The iron is in my soul and on my stomach. I can only eat when I can see the sunshine again.'

'Well, you'll not see the sunshine again, not ever,' Feargal retorted. 'And if you don't want to die, you'd better eat, sunshine or no!'

She WILL see the sunshine, and soon, I thought angrily.

'Well, I'll fetch you food no matter what you say. I will not have Lord Conor saying that I have starved you to death. I will tell him it is your own stubbornness that made you die, I shall so. If you go and be inconvenient and die, it will be your own fault entirely, and none at all of mine.'

Nest wearily closed her eyes again.

Feargal Shamrock bustled out, closing the door and dropping the heavy bolt across, and I scuttled across the earth floor towards Nest, T.A. and O'Liam hard upon what would have been my heels if I hadn't been an ant.

Swiftly, before the dreadful iron chains had the chance to affect me, I shifted us back, and then, careful to hold T.A.'s body as a shield between me and the chains, I called to Nest, softly. Her eyes shot open and she struggled to sit up. The chains clanked, and I saw that they had rubbed at the skin of her ankles and wrists so much that it was raw and bleeding. T.A. tried to pull away from me to go to her, but I held her back. 'Don't move, T.A.,' I said softly, 'I can't be exposed to the iron so soon after the last time,' and she kept still, obediently covering me.

'Tansy!' Nest whispered, hardly able to believe her eyes. 'It's you! But where's Gwydion?'

'Gwydion's still in Ynys Haf,' I said. 'He was wounded, Nest, but don't worry, he's well on his way to recovery. He just isn't well enough to ride heroically to the rescue on his white horse yet, so you'll have to make do with me, I'm afraid!' I grinned at her. 'O'Liam,' I said, turning to the little man, 'do you think you can talk those chains into disappearing?'

O'Liam strutted over to Nest and kicked a loop of chain. 'Oh, I can so, Lady. Didn't I find this very iron myself? Didn't I tame it after a long struggle until it would do EXACTLY as I want? Am I not O'Liam of the Green Boots, Ironfinder and Chief Leprechaun to the Dragonking of Ynys Haf? Am I not –'

'Yes, you are, O'Liam,' I said, 'but Feargal Shamrock will be back soon, and I'd really like to get us all out of here before he arrived.'

'Oh. Oh yes, ah, right.' O'Liam folded his arms and glared at the chains. 'I thought I'd trained you better than this, iron!' he said sternly. 'I don't care if you HAVE been through a terrible ordeal by fire that melted you altogether. You are still MY iron and you will do what I say!'

The chains rattled nervously.

'Right,' O'Liam said, 'there's a gap beneath the door big enough for you to go through. Will you take yourselves off, this instant, before I lose my temper entirely with you?' He bent forward, menacingly. 'Or will you stay and see what I myself, O'Liam Ironfinder, will do to you?'

The chains rattled like a houseful of ghosts. The bands holding Nest's wrists opened, and the chains began to wriggle noisily, like a long, clumsy snake, towards the door.

'And don't be hanging around out there when I come through that door,' O'Liam called as they disappeared, 'or it will be the worse for you entirely, so it will!' The reply from the tunnel outside sounded as if the chains had decided to run.

Nest rubbed her wrists and winced.

'I'll fix those when we get you out of here,' I assured her. 'Can you walk?'

Nest tried to stand up, but her legs collapsed beneath her. 'I'm sorry,' she said, shoving her dark hair out of her eyes, 'I've been here too long. Too close to the iron.'

Suddenly I heard a noise outside. 'Feargal! Quick, Nest,' I whispered, 'lie down again.' I changed T.A. and O'Liam back into ants, and then shifted myself. The door opened and there was Feargal, bending down to pick up a tray of food from the earth floor.

'Now, fairy,' he puffed, chugging across the floor with the tray. 'If I help you, will you eat a bit, at all?'

Nest said nothing, just looked at him coldly.

'Ah, you will,' he wheedled, 'for if you do not you will die, and then where will you be?'

Behind his back I silently shifted into myself, and stood behind him leaning against the wall, my arms folded. I could hardly wait for him to turn and see me. I wanted to see him jump.

Feargal picked up a piece of bread and held it out to Nest. Silently she took it. Just as Feargal noticed that his prisoner had somehow managed not only to unchain herself but lose the chains as well, she tossed the bread high over his head and I caught it in mid-air. Feargal spun round like a top.

And fainted.

I was quite disappointed. I had several really good sarcastic remarks ready to use on him, but they would be completely wasted on somebody who was unconscious. I shifted the others back, and O'Liam prodded the heap of leprechaun with the toe of his emerald boot.

'Ha!' he said mockingly. 'Did you think you could use my iron for your own purposes, Feargal Shamrock? Because no matter what you use it for, it is still mine, so there, so it is!'

Feargal Shamrock groaned as he regained consciousness. He didn't open his eyes before he spoke. 'Is it yourself, O'Liam?' he asked, his voice weak, 'If it is, and I am not hearing ghosties, what might you be doing here?'

'It is me, myself. And regarding what I might be doing here, mind your own business, Feargal Shamrock.'

'Well, for the sake of old times, O'Liam, will you tell me is the fairy free of her iron chains, or am I imagining the very thing?'

'Sure and you aren't blessed with that much imagination,' O'Liam mocked. 'Lady Nest is free entirely, and now we shall take her. I wish I could stay behind to hear you explain that to Lord Conor, but I do not think it would be wise to do so at all.'

Feargal Shamrock's eyes popped open. 'Ah, can you not leave a little bit of her behind? Just a wee, wee little piece? A foot maybe? Or even a finger? Conor will be beside himself with rage if she is gone altogether, and a wee bit of her might be enough to stop his rage. If you will not, I shall be a sorry leprechaun. If he lets me live,' he finished miserably.

Good! I thought, remembering how he had shut Nest up in the deepest dungeon in the Land Beneath. *Serves you right.*

'We need every bit of the Lady Nest,' O'Liam told him. 'And if Conor splodges you underfoot like a spider, it will be your own fault.'

'If I were you, Feargal Shamrock,' T.A. put in, 'I'd make myself scarce. I wouldn't hang around to give Conor the bad news. Why go looking for trouble?'

'Why indeed?' Feargal said thoughtfully. 'You speak a great big bit of sense, there, Lady. Tell me now, if I was to take myself off right away at once, would you be after stopping me at all?'

I looked at T.A. and Nest. Both of them shook their heads. 'Go now, or you'll be sorry,' I threatened. 'And don't come back. Ever!'

I didn't have to tell him twice. The leprechaun was off and out of the door in a flash. I heard his feet pounding on the packed earth of the tunnel. I doubt if he stopped before he was twenty miles away!

'Ooh, I'm such a big old softie!' I said. 'I should have turned him into a slug and put salt on him.'

'No, you shouldn't.' T.A. punched me gently on the arm. 'You're still a nice-ish person, even if you are the Lady of Ynys Haf.'

'What do you mean, "nice-ish"?' I said indignantly.

'Stop it, you two.' Nest was trying to struggle to her feet again. 'The most important thing is that we get out of here, fix me up, and then decide what we are going to do next.'

Personally, I thought it would be a good idea to take Nest and head back for Ynys Haf. Conor of the Land Beneath could whistle for Maebh, AND O'Liam for that matter. And then I remembered that we still had to find Siobhan Flowerface for O'Liam, and that unless I kept my promise to Conor and managed to talk him out of wanting Maebh and O'Liam back, Ynys Haf would still be caught in the dreadful cycle of hot, dry weather that was killing our lovely land. Add to that Rhiryd ap Rhiryd and his brothers and the mercenaries still infesting the Island of Summer, and the Oldway Creatures still loose and dangerous – not to mention my invisible enemy, Master Henbane. If I didn't sort all of that out, nothing would be solved at all.

But first, we had to get out of the Land Beneath. I peered out of the door. The tunnel was clear in both directions. 'Can you walk, Nest?'

'I think so.'

With me in the lead, and the others following, we crept along the tunnel, listening hard at every bend to make sure that no one was coming towards us. Once we got to the door that led to the more pleasant parts of the Land Beneath, I shifted us all once more into ants, and we scuttled beneath it.

We kept to the edge of the corridors, and steadily climbed up and up, avoiding feet, until we were out once more and in the fresh air. I didn't risk changing us back right away. I wanted to get well away from Conor and the Land Beneath first.

And that was how we almost lost T.A…

14

We were scuttling along being ants, all our six little legs shuttling madly, galloping over leaves and twigs, trying to put as much distance between us and the Land Beneath as we could. T.A. was in the lead; she seemed to have got the feel of having six legs very quickly (well YOU try it! It isn't as easy as it sounds, you know) and she was a metre or so in front of us. I was trying to keep an eye on O'Liam and Nest: O'Liam couldn't co-ordinate his third and fifth legs and kept tripping over them, and Nest was still weak after being shut up for so long.

I glanced up just in time to see a humungous (well, I was an ant at the time, remember?) black and white shape swoop down from the sky like a guided missile. It was a magpie, and it was heading straight for T.A.

'Look out!' I yelled, 'Duck!'

O'Liam looked up. 'Ah, that's no duck, Lady,' he began, and then realised what I was on about and dived under a dead leaf.

Fortunately T.A. was paying attention, and she lost no time in hurling herself beneath the leaf-mould that carpeted the forest floor. The magpie searched about for a while, turning over dead leaves and peering beneath them, hopefully, with its bright black eyes.

I shoved Nest under a twig for safety, and hid myself behind an acorn. And then the magpie twitched, and its outline shimmered hazily, and suddenly – there was Maebh, all by herself in the middle of the forest, with her back to me.

Gotcha!

In a trice I had shifted myself back, frantically searching my memory for the right spell. I had it, and I zapped her with it. She shimmered again, and at my feet was a large hedgepig. It turned round, saw me, and rolled crossly into a tight ball, its prickles sticking out threateningly.

I magicked myself a string bag, and rolled Maebh into it. I picked her up and dangled her in front of my nose. I knew she didn't have enough magical powers to get herself out of the hedgehog shape I'd put her into.

'Right, Maebh!' I said happily, 'I think it's time you paid a visit to Ynys Haf while I decide what I'm going to do about you!'

She didn't unroll.

I lifted the twigs and stuff that O'Liam and T.A. were cowering beneath, shifted them back, and grinned.

'We've got Maebh,' I said, waving the hedgehog, 'we've rescued Nest, and now I suggest we get back to Ynys Haf and decide what we're going to do next!'

I shifted us all into golden eagles and we soared up, up into the afternoon sky, me carrying the string bag with Maebh in it. She was still rolled up. I think she might have been sulking. Once at the coast, we landed on a lonely, rocky shore and I shifted all of us – except Maebh, of course – back to our own shapes.

'How shall we travel?' I asked. 'Nest, if I make you a gull or a gannet, do you think you could make it across the water?'

She shook her head. 'I don't think so. I feel so weak, Tansy. I've been struggling to keep up with the rest of you just this little distance from the Land Beneath. I'll never be able to make it across the sea.'

I'd been afraid of that. I sighed. There was nothing else for it then. It would have to be a boat. The trouble was, I just didn't think that I could bear to cross the Middlesome Sea in a boat ever again. T.A. was looking at me hopefully.

'???' the expression said. I grinned. I knew exactly what she had in mind.

First of all I magicked a boat, just big enough to take a leprechaun, a hedgepig and a half-fairy, pushed it into the sea until it was bobbing inshore, and let the others climb in. Then T.A. and I waded out up to our waists and shifted us both into dolphins.

Now, if there is anything at all that I would rather be if I couldn't be me, it would have to be a dolphin. We were bottle-noses, and T.A. and I swam madly out to sea and jumped for the joy of it, arcing up into the blue sky and splashing down, chasing a stream of bright bubbles back up to the surface, the icy water chill on our sleek skins. I admit, we showed off a bit before swimming back to the boat and taking the twin tow-ropes at the bow end in our mouths and heading for home.

We discovered that we could make the boat fairly dance along behind us, and we could have been back in Ynys Haf in record time. But then I glanced over my shoulder and saw that O'Liam was hanging over the back of the boat being sea-sick, and Nest was looking fairly greenish too. So we slowed down to a less lively pace, and it was obviously a more comfortable ride for them, because O'Liam stopped throwing up.

It was a long swim, even for dolphins, and my shoulder muscles were hurting by the time the great sweep of Gwyddno Garanhir's sea-wall hove into view (see how sea-faring I'm getting?). The vast sluice-gates were open to the incoming tide, and T.A. and I nosed the little boat into the harbour and up against the harbour wall. Nest managed to tie the boat to a huge ring while I shifted T.A. and I back to ourselves. We swam to the harbour steps and climbed up them. Nest gathered up the string bag with Maebh in it and helped O'Liam up the steps.

'Oh, Lady, I don't think I am at all a sea-going style of Leprechaun!' O'Liam groaned. 'Not while all the time it is going up and down and down and up in a wholly unsympathetic and unreasonable way.' He tottered along the quay. 'And now the earth is doing altogether the same thing!' he complained, and sat down on a lobster-pot.

'You'll feel better soon,' I promised, 'when you've got some food inside you.'

O'Liam looked doubtful. 'I don't think I will ever eat again, Lady,' he said. 'For isn't the stomach in me going round and round all the while the rest of me is travelling up and down?'

Personally, I doubted that O'Liam would never eat again. All I'd have to do would be to wave some chips under his nose, and a bottle of tomato sauce, and he'd be elbow deep.

The sluice-gate keeper, Seithennyn, was judging the height of the incoming tide, getting ready to close the gates of Cantre'r Gwaelod at exactly the right time. He gave us a wave as he began to turn the great wheel that pulled the ropes that closed the gates against the sea. I gave him a Hard Stare. That's the trouble with knowing a legend like that one: it's like waiting for the other shoe to drop!

King Gwyddno was eating his lunch when we got up to his palace, but he welcomed us as he always did, getting a servant to set extra places at his table, and sending another scurrying to the kitchens to fetch food for us. O'Liam, I was not surprised to see, fell upon the food when it came like a starving man. I parked the hedgepig under my chair and made sure I got my share before he demolished it all.

Gwyddno's wife, who was Nest's distant cousin, took her away as soon as she'd eaten to bandage up the raw places on her wrists and ankles where the vicious iron shackles had cut into her. O'Liam curled up on a pile of cushions in a corner and fell fast asleep, and T.A. made her excuses and wandered off to see if she could find Elffin, Gwyddno's son, for whom she definitely has a Soft Spot. Which left me with King Gwyddno.

The trouble, as I mentioned before, with having foreknowledge when Something Terrible is going to happen, like the drowning of Cantre'r Gwaelod and all its people, is that I have this very, very strong compulsion to at least give the people concerned a bit of a hint. I kept having this terrible feeling that the minute I turned my back it would probably happen, and I'd never forgive myself if they all died. Merlin, Taliesin and Gwydion would probably collectively marmalize me if they found out, and Flissy and Nest would be furious. But I had to give a little hint, right?

'Gwyddno,' I began, 'that sea wall of yours?'

'Mmm?' he said absent-mindedly, reading through a great pile of parchments that a clerk had left in front of him.

'Well, I've been wondering how safe it is.' I couldn't just come right out with it and say, 'Hey, you're all gonna die if you don't listen to me,' could I?

'What?' he peered at me. He had little round spectacles that I suspected Merlin might have brought back for him from an optician in another Time, and his eyes were very blue over the rims of them. 'Safe? The wall?'

'Mm.'

'Oh, don't trouble your little head about that, Tanith dear! It's as solid as a rock. My great-great-grandad built that a couple of centuries ago, and we've never had a drop of flood-water in Cantre'r Gwaelod since. I get it checked once every six months, right after the equinoctial tides, just to make certain there's been no damage.'

The trouble was, I knew that the problem wasn't the wall. It was the keeper. 'But what about Seithennyn?'

'Him? Oh, he's a good man. Very trustworthy. Been at the job since his old Dad passed on twenty years ago, and there's his son Einion ready to take over when he pops off, which he won't for ages yet, I hope. No problems there, either.'

I had to ask, didn't I? 'Are you planning any parties, Gwyddno?'

And then a familiar voice burst into the conversation. 'Good heavens! Is that Tanith's voice?'

I swung round. 'Taliesin! What are you doing here?'

'Visiting,' he said pointedly, 'and it's probably just as well that I am. Your mouth could run for Wales in the Olympics, Tanith. And it's just as well I arrived when I did.'

I tried to be nonchalant. 'Oh, really? Why would that be?'

He grinned, knowing perfectly well that I was pretending to be innocent. 'Because your hedgehog is making a break for freedom.'

He was right. Maebh had managed to get her four stubby little feet through the holes in the string bag and was making her way determinedly towards the door like a travelling fishing net. I wasn't quite sure how she thought she was going to manage the spiral stairs of the tower, but I caught her before she got there anyway.

'Oops! Thanks, Taliesin.'

He raised an eyebrow. 'Glad I got here in time to save the day, Tanz. Goodness knows what might have happened if I'd arrived a bit later.'

I knew perfectly well that he didn't mean the hedgehog.

'When did you take up hedgehog collecting?' he enquired.

'This morning. In Ireland. It's Maebh, by the way.'

'Is it indeed? I thought she was in Erin.'

I realised then that he didn't have a clue what had been happening in Ynys Haf. He'd been gadding about with Merlin again. What was it he'd been doing? Oh, right, I remembered. He'd gone off to sort out King Arthur and Guinevere. 'Taliesin, there's quite a lot you don't know.'

'I doubt that,' he said, smugly.

'Know-all!' I retorted. 'Did you know that Conor of the Land Beneath has attacked Ynys Haf with loads of mercenaries, and has taken Castell Du?'

He nodded.

'Oh. Well, did you know that the Oldway Creatures are loose?'

He nodded.

'Did you know that Gwydion has been wounded?'

He nodded. 'He's getting better, though,' he said calmly.

'Yes. But did you know that Master Henbane is back, and he's invisible still, and he's out to get me? And take over Ynys Haf again?'

He nodded. 'Of course,' he said. 'People like him don't give up easily. And if, as you say, Maebh is still about, then of course Henbane will be, too. Merlin told you that making an enemy invisible was not a particularly bright thing to do.'

'Oh,' I said again. 'Did you know that Ynys Haf is dying of drought because Conor – at least, I *think* it's Conor – has done something to the weather?'

He hadn't known that.

'Now that IS serious,' he said thoughtfully. 'Merlin must know about this straight away.'

'What?' I was flabbergasted. 'You mean you've known all about the other problems I've been having and you haven't done anything to help?'

He stared at me. 'Of course not! It was your job – well, yours and Gwydion's – to sort out all the little snags and hiccups. I knew you'd do it. It was your fault, anyway, making a promise like that to Conor of the Land Beneath and not keeping it. Of course he's ratty with you. You just can't go about making promises and not keeping them. You're the Lady of Ynys Haf, Tan'ith, and you have to take responsibility for what happens to its people.'

I opened and shut my mouth. I must have looked like a goldfish. 'Let me get this straight,' I said at last, as evenly as I could, because I was having a bit of a job keeping my temper. 'You knew all about the problems Gwydion has had, right?'

He nodded.

'And sorting out everything that's happened is down to me and Gwydion, right?'

He nodded.

'But when I mention that Ynys Haf itself is in trouble, that's really serious, right?'

He looked at me blankly. 'Well, of course!'

'Why?' I burst out furiously. 'Why just the land?'

'I would have thought that was obvious, since you know Merlin. Ynys Haf and her people belong to Gwydion and to you while you are here. But Merlin – and to a lesser degree, I – have a view of the larger picture. Merlin's first priority is the Island of Summer. She must go on into the future, whatever happens to you and Gwydion. Otherwise your Time will never happen.'

I had no answer to that. The whole idea of a future without us in it was too huge to imagine. Gwydion and I were only important as temporary keepers of Ynys Haf. Merlin would go on forever, to make certain that Ynys Haf, in whatever form, did also.

15

We were back in Ynys Haf by nightfall, and Taliesin was with us. I was quite glad that he came too. That way I knew that Cantre'r Gwaelod was safe for a while, at least, because it couldn't drown unless he was there, according to the legend.

As soon as we got there, I handed Maebh over to Aunty Fliss, who found a wooden cage to put her in, and fed her some bread and milk for supper.

Gwydion was asleep when we arrived, Bran and Garan the wolfhounds stretched out alongside him. They lolloped over and sniffed and licked us comprehensively, and then went back to guarding Gwydion. Aunty Fliss said that he was recovering fast – fast enough to be thoroughly tetchy and bad-tempered most of the time. He was able to walk a little way, and the wound in his side was almost completely healed, now.

However, he was very fed up with living in the mountains in a camp when Rhiryd Goch and a load of foreigners were living in his castle and probably messing it up. He felt a bit better when I dangled Maebh-the-Hedgehog in front of his nose, and better still when he discovered that Taliesin was close behind me.

'About time you showed up,' he grumbled. 'I don't suppose Merlin's bothered to pitch up as well?'

'Merlin's still having problems with Arthur and Guinevere,' Taliesin said, moving a shortsword and a pile of manuscripts so that he could sit down on the end of Gwydion's mattress. 'Arthur's discovered a son he didn't know he had and Guinevere's taken a fancy to that swollen-headed idiot Lancelot. He'll be there a while longer, I dare say, so it's up to us to sort out Ynys Haf. It's no good hanging around waiting for him.'

'There's so much to sort out I don't know where to start,' Gwydion scratched his head. 'And it's hot in this stupid tent. And we wouldn't be in this mess if Tanith hadn't gone and got Conor of the Land Beneath all riled up, and –'

'Oh, stop complaining,' I retorted. 'I've brought back Maebh, haven't I? And rescued Nest? Which is more than you've done.'

'I've been wounded, haven't I?' he said with an air of being very offended. 'If I'd been fit none of this would have happened.'

I raised my eyes heaven-ward. 'Instead of whinging at me, shouldn't you be thinking about what we're going to do next?'

He sniffed. 'What are you asking me for? I thought you were taking over. You're so good at it, apparently.'

Taliesin looked from Gwydion to me and back again. 'Come on, you two,' he said. 'Arguing won't get us anywhere. Gwydion, you're ratty because you are in pain and frustrated at not being able to get out of here, and Tanith's ratty because she's tired – and probably hungry, if I know her. Come on, Gwyd, you can hop outside even if you can't walk properly yet. I smell venison cooking and I think it would be a good plan if we got at it before O'Liam does.'

He helped Gwydion to stand up, found him the wooden branch he was using as a sort of crutch, and held the tent flap back for him to struggle out. The air outside was fresher with the coming of the darkness, and the smell of woodsmoke and roasting meat tickled my nose and made me realise how hungry I was.

We sat around the fire and ate and drank, and because it was a special occasion, being all together again, and because I felt guilty at being argumentative with Gwydion, I magicked us all chocolate fudge cake – hot – for pudding. O'Liam almost fainted with ecstasy.

'Oooh, Lady,' was all he could say. He licked his bowl clean, and fell asleep where he sat, chocolate all over his pointed golden face. He even had a blob on the end of his nose. Bran was sniffing around it hopefully. I hoped he didn't take it into his head to lick it off, because if O'Liam woke up and saw that hairy great lump looming over him, he'd probably have the leprechaun equivalent of a heart attack!

Taliesin slipped away after a while, and so did Fliss, Nest and T.A., leaving just Gwydion and me alone – except for about two dozen of Gwydion's men-at-arms here and there in the camp, as well as the watchmen at the entrance to the secret place in the mountain.

We sat close together, and after a while, he said, softly, 'Sorry, Tanz.'

It was on the tip of my tongue to say 'So I should think!' but common sense kicked in (there you are! I HAVE got some, after all!), so I didn't. Instead, I said 'That's all right, Gwydion. It must be terrible for you to be stuck here and not be able to do anything.'

His arm crept round me, and I felt his chin on top of my head. I leaned back against him, comfortably, taking care not to put too much pressure on his wound. I could feel how much weight he'd lost, and it worried me. No wonder he was bad-tempered and frustrated. We sat that way, companionably, until one of the men came to build up the fire for the night, and then we said goodnight and went to our separate tents. I was glad we were friends again.

I slept really well, despite T.A. snoring like a pig. Next morning we woke up again to bright sunlight and heat, and breakfasted on bacon and eggs that I magicked after taking one look at the wrinkled, soft apples which were all that was left to eat in the camp – apart from venison soup, which I didn't particularly fancy for breakfast, thank you very much.

When we'd eaten, we got together in the shade of the tree: Taliesin, Gwydion, Nest, Flissy, T.A., O'Liam and me. We needed to discuss our plan of action, and the more brains there were to work on it, the better, because everybody knows mine aren't up to much on their own!

Gwydion acted as the sort of chairman, being Dragonking. He leaned against the tree-trunk and looked round at us all. 'Right,' he began. 'What have we still got to do?'

'Less than we had last time we met, thanks to Tansy,' Nest said, smiling at me gratefully.

'But there's still a lot to be done.' Taliesin was shredding a blade of yellowing grass. 'We need to get rid of Rhiryd ap Rhiryd Goch and his mercenaries, hunt down the Oldway Creatures and get them turned back to stone –' he glanced at the ugly great stone creature that was still occupying a large part of the camp '– as the Lady, that's Tanith's job, I think.'

'Thanks a bunch,' I grumbled, but I knew he was right. I wasn't looking forward to doing it, though.

'And when we've done that we should be able to turn our attention to Conor of the Land Beneath. Now we have Maebh, we can hand her over and get him to remove whatever enchantment he's put on Ynys Haf. With any luck he'll agree to O'Liam staying here – he's a free leprechaun, after all, because he's been away from the Land Beneath for three full moons and three full days. Once that's sorted, we'll be back to normal, and we can all get on with our lives, right? It will all be over.'

O'Liam was tugging frantically at my sleeve, and I remembered. 'There is just one other thing,' I put in.

'What?' Gwydion's brows drew together in a frown. 'What else is wrong?'

'Nothing. But O'Liam wants us to get his lady friend out of the Land Beneath.'

Gwydion sighed. 'That could complicate matters. Is it absolutely necessary?'

T.A., Nest, Flissy and I spoke with one voice. 'Of course it is!'

Gwydion looked taken aback. 'Oh. Serious, is it?'

O'Liam blushed. 'Oh, it is so, your Dragon-kingship. Siobhan Flowerface is the sun in my sky, the full moon in my dark night, the flowers that grow in the spring, the red tomatoey stuff on my chippety things –'

Gwydion held up his hand, laughing. 'I get the picture, O'Liam. Well, we'll do our best to get her out for you. We may have to kidnap her, but if she wants to come, that shouldn't be a problem. But first –'

'The Oldway Creatures,' I said, miserably. 'Down to me, right?'

Then T.A. put her hand up. 'Look,' she said, 'I know I'm not magical like you lot are. Well, not very. I've only got the little bit that was lent to me the first time I came to Ynys Haf. But I had a thought last night. I wondered if the Oldway Creatures couldn't possibly be – well, turned?'

'Turned?' I said doubtfully, 'what, you mean turn them round and march them into the sea or something? No, that wouldn't work.'

She gazed at me exasperatedly. 'No, you dingbat. If we marched them into the sea they'd just turn round and march back again, right? And be twice as ratty as before. No, what I mean is, maybe somewhere there's a spell that can change them from the Other Side, to ours. They belong in Ynys Haf, don't they? They weren't brought here by the Great Druid from somewhere else?'

I shook my head. 'No. I think Merlin said they've always been here. Sort of remnants of the prehistoric age in Ynys Haf. Why?'

'Because I thought – well, if we could turn them onto our side, we could use them to help us get rid of Rhiryd ap Rhiryd and his collection of horribles down at Castell y Ddraig, right?'

I stared at her. 'It's a nice idea. Trouble is, I can't actually think of any spell right now – but give me a while to try to remember the Spellorium and maybe I can come up with something.'

'Not only the Spellorium, Tanith,' Nest reminded me. 'You have the Lady's magic, too. The Oldway

Creatures belong in Ynys Haf – perhaps she had a spell to control them.'

Something small and vaguely intelligent was glimmering at the back of my brain. 'Do you know,' I said, after a little think, 'you may have a point, there!'

Gwydion went to have a nap, O'Liam went in search of elevenses, T.A. and Nest and Flissy went to organise various things around the camp, and I sat under the tree and went over my collection of spells and magic abilities in my head. I closed my eyes and called up the Spellorium. That's the good bit about being a witch: you can memorise entire spell-books, and recall them, the way you'd call up a document on your computer. Tends to give me a bit of a headache if I do it for too long, but then, so does revising maths. This time I had the answer within an hour. Just in time for lunch, in fact.

Which was cold venison sandwiches. We all gathered under the tree again, and Flissy handed them round. O'Liam stared at his plate as if there was something missing. He glanced up at me, his huge eyes appealing. I'm not stupid. I can take a hint. Cold venison sandwiches – and chips. Oh, and tomato ketchup. Sir Walter Raleigh had better get a move on and discover the potato if only for O'Liam's sake! He was a chip-junkie if ever I saw one.

And when our lunch had gone down, we went in search of the remaining five Oldway Creatures. At least, I hoped there were only five. As far as I could remember, there had only been six in the cave the last time I'd battled with them. Or was it seven? I racked my brain to remember, but it had been working hard and was tired.

Taliesin came with me: we left the others behind for safety. The easiest way to find them was to search from the air, so we shifted into seagulls, spread our strong wings and took to the skies. We started at the cave, and moved inland. I hoped they wouldn't be far from the mountains: the thought of having to search the whole of Ynys Haf, North, South, East and West, was a bit depressing.

We swooped over the edge of the cliff and down to the apron of shingle in front of their cave, which was empty except for huge footprints – oh, and the snoring form of the Great Druid, asleep on his rock where I'd left him a year or so back. At least I didn't have to worry about him at the moment. He wasn't much to worry about, admittedly – he was more a poser with a bit of magic than anything else – but I could do without any more problems, thank you very much.

We flew along the shoreline for a while, skimming the white-topped waves, but there was no sign of the Oldway Creatures. So we set off inland, swooping over the empty shell that was Castell Du, glancing into the courtyard in case any of the creatures were there.

Beyond the castle, at the edge of the woods the village: empty houses and smokeless roof-holes, deserted pathways – and an Oldway Creature, tramping away from the village towards the mountains, shoving into trees like a football hooligan in a crowd. We swooped ahead of it and waited for it to come closer.

'What are you going to do, Tanz?' Taliesin squawked.

'There's a spell that just might work.' I stretched my wings and folded them again. 'I've never tried it before, and it's supposed to work with savage creatures of any sort – but I don't think it's ever been tried on an Oldway before. But hey, try anything once, right?' I probably sounded lots braver than I felt.

The creature was massive: much bigger than when I'd first encountered it in the sea-cave so long ago. It had a long, thick tail with triangular jagged bits sticking up the back, and a point on the end, strong hind legs and shorter front legs – or maybe arms, since it was walking along upright, snapping off bits of tree-top and chucking them about. It wasn't eating them, though. It was too much to hope for that it was a herbivore. Nothing with teeth like that could possibly be anything other than a thoroughly enthusiastic carnivore! As well as the teeth – a full set of molars plus two long fangs each in its top and bottom jaws – it had two sharp horns sticking out of its head.

And I was going to reason with it?

16

Well, no, actually, I wasn't. Going to reason with it, I mean. I was going to try to put a spell on it. The only trouble was that I couldn't stay a seagull *and* perform the spell. I had to change back to me, Tan'ith the witch, to do it. I thought it might be a good idea to shift modestly (and unobtrusively) behind a tree. A big tree…

I found a large oak growing a little way ahead of the Creature, flew behind it, landed on the ground, shimmered and flexed into my own body. I wiggled my shoulder-blades, getting them comfortable after being wings. Bits of me grumble a bit, because I use muscles I don't usually have, when I shift. If you see what I mean. Well, I know what I mean, anyway.

I waited until the Creature was demolishing a silver birch a few yards away, stepped silently out from behind the tree, and considered the best way of getting its attention so that I could zap it. That was the trouble with this particular spell. You had to make eye contact with the subject, or it wouldn't work. Sounds a load of fun, right? Not.

I cleared my throat, but the Creature was too busy ripping birch roots out of the ground to notice. 'Oi, lizard chops!' I bellowed at last. 'Have you got a minute?'

It stopped demolishing the shrubbery and slowly turned to face me. Its little red, piggy eyes glared at me disbelievingly. I looked it right in the eyes and chucked the spell.

Unfortunately, it didn't work. It bounced off the hard,

bony scales in the middle of its forehead, between the horns. Oops. Then it lowered its head, licked its scaly lips and decided to eat me. Now, there was no way I was hanging around for that to happen. I'm quite partial to my various bits and pieces, and I like them the way they are, right? I'm sort of attached to them and I want them to stay that way. So I ran. And as I ran I thought, furiously. There had to be a way of getting the spell into it. Some way into its tiny brain that bypassed the bony plates of its stupid skull. Then I stopped thinking, furiously or otherwise, and did a jump that would have put Colin Jackson to shame, because a VERY LARGE head with ENORMOUS teeth had just appeared in front of me, upside down. It had caught up with me, and was looming over the top of me. I turned round and backed away, and the creature turned its head the right way up and slobbered a bit.

If I stayed where I was, the very large teeth attached to the very large head would bite me, and I didn't like that idea much. So I jumped up onto its head and hung on to the horns for dear life, feeling like whatsisname, John Wayne, in one of those old cowboy pictures, riding a bucking bronco.

The Creature twirled, twisted, shook its head up and down and bounced like Tigger to shake me off.

'Aaaaah!' I screamed loudly, except it came out like 'A-ugh-a-ugh-a-ugh,' what with the bounces. And then one of the bounces must have shaken a brain cell into life. I wrapped both my legs round the Creature's neck, slithered my top half down between its eyes, which rather surprised it, because its eyes crossed, and shoved the spell right up its nose. Then I clamped my hands over its rather snotty snitch to make sure it didn't sneeze it out again, even though this put my very valuable fingers rather too close for comfort to those extraordinarily large choppers.

The Creature bucked and snorted for a while, and then, quite suddenly, stopped. It stood still. I waited for a while, in case the spell hadn't taken properly, but it seemed to have worked, so I slithered shakily down its neck and plopped onto the ground beside it.

Taliesin flew down and shifted, and the Creature sat back on its haunches and smirked dopily at us. Then it put out about a metre of red tongue and slurped me affectionately, which was most unpleasant. I don't think it had Macleaned its teeth for about six months.

'Ugh! Gerroff!' I said, shoving its head aside. It looked hurt, but then obviously forgave me, and nuzzled me lovingly. Trouble is, a nuzzle from something the size of a single-decker bus can be a bit overwhelming. When I picked myself up from twelve metres away, and Taliesin stopped chortling, I shook my finger at the beast. 'Cut that out, OK? I know you're my new buddy, but I'll do the cuddling, right?'

The Oldway Creature put its head on one side. I think it understood. The question was, what did we do with it while we tracked down the other – four, was it? In the end we decided Taliesin would take it back to the camp while I went hunting for the others. It ambled obediently off behind him, glancing lovingly at me over its shoulder as it went. Its expression said, sort of 'missing you already'. Yuk. I shifted back to seagull, and took off again.

I found the next one about a mile away, and then

two together a few hundred yards east of that one. I zapped the solo one first, and then waited until the other two were separated by a clump of trees before fixing them both singly. I got them together in a little group and told them to sit and wait. They sat quietly like large, obedient puppies, while I went looking for the fourth, and final one. That made five live ones, and the stone one back at camp made six, which was the whole lot, as far as I could remember.

The last one was slightly different from the others. It had wings, but they were more ornamental than useful, because they were stubby little leathery ones that flapped a lot and made a cool breeze, but would never have got him off the ground no matter how hard he waved them around. I zapped him, too, and led him back to the other three. Then, with the four Creatures following me like over-large domestic cows following an extremely small dairymaid, I set off for the mountains.

The weather was so hot that it felt like walking through an oven. There was hardly a blade of grass to be seen anywhere, all the wildflowers were dead, and the bushes and trees had a parched look. One spark and the whole countryside would go up like a torch. The stream beds were either dry or reduced to a thin, greenish trickle and the dead bodies of frogs and fish littered the dried banks.

We walked and walked, the Oldway Creatures lumbering docilely and slowly because of the heat. I hitched a lift on one when we got to the foot of Snowdon: it was a long climb and I was thirsty.

We created quite a stir in the camp when we

arrived. The big Creature with the wings went and sniffed at the stone one in the middle of the clearing, and nudged it with its nose. It rocked, but it didn't fall over, and the creature lost interest and ambled away. I magicked a large stone bath full of water and a vast pile of raw sausages (I couldn't bring myself to produce great big hunks of raw cow for some reason. I know sausages are cow-and-pig too, but I never said I was logical, did I?) Anyway, the Oldway Creatures were very grateful. They snuffled at the bangers for a while and then demolished them, slurping up the strings like pink spaghetti, emptied the bath with five almighty noses giving five almighty slurps, nestled in a heap like giant puppies, and went to sleep. They were quite sweet, really. If you like your pets bus-sized, with horns and fangs and talons!

'There,' I said, in a self-satisfied sort of manner, 'that's sorted out the Oldway Creatures. Now tomorrow we can go and get rid of Rhiryd ap Rhiryd Goch, and his nasty little brothers.'

T.A. was counting heads and tails. 'One, two, three, four, five – and the frozen one makes six,' she muttered. 'Is that all, Tanz?'

'Is that all?' I spluttered. 'Isn't that enough? Good grief, T.A., I'd like to have seen you tackle this lot!'

'What I mean is, I'm sure there were seven, originally,' she said. 'I've got this picture in my mind's eye, that's all. And my picture says seven Oldway Creatures. Not six.'

'No,' I said crossly. 'The picture in MY head says six. And six is plenty. Definitely six. Right, Taliesin?'

Taliesin closed his eyes and thought. 'I can't be

certain,' he confessed. 'Either of you could be right. But we've got six, and the remaining one – if there is another out there somewhere – shouldn't be much trouble even if we do run into it. Not now we know how to handle them. Right, Tanz?'

'Right. But it's definitely six, not seven.'

T.A. shrugged, but I could see she still wasn't convinced. 'If you say so. But –'

I wasn't listening.

It was so hot that night that we couldn't bear to be inside the tents. Ynys Haf seemed to be getting hotter and hotter, and even though Nest and Flissy had been hard at work all day to try to change the weather, whatever spell Conor seemed to have put on it seemed to be firmly stuck. Even within our mountain sanctuary the ground was beginning to crack like crazy-paving. The air was absolutely still, and the heat was hot and dry, like sitting under a hair-dryer.

The sky was clear, with not a hint of cloud obscuring the stars. I had forgotten how lovely stars are when there is no pollution to hide them. The sky seemed low, and the brilliant points of light twinkled, apparently so near that I felt that I could reach out and pick them like ripe blackberries. There was a slim fingernail crescent of moon, but no haze that might mean that welcome rain was coming. It felt as if it would never rain or be cool again.

On the other side of the camp the heap of Oldway Creatures twitched and snored, and Gwydion slept with his great dogs at his side. Although Gwydion was sleeping outside, as we were, O'Liam was still guarding Gwydion's tent door, the emerald boots placed neatly beside him. I gazed affectionately at his humped shape and decided that next time he needed boots I might magic him a pair of bright green trainers – with flashing lights in the soles. He'd love those!

I was just about dropping off to sleep, gazing at the hypnotic banks of stars, picking out the Great Bear, the Milky Way (actually, I haven't got a clue what they look like, but I try to imagine, OK?) when suddenly I realised that the sky was getting dark. Bit by bit the stars were being hidden. I thought at first, hopefully, that it was cloud, but it was darker and heavier than cloud. I nudged T.A. awake, and crawled across to Gwydion.

'Gwyd! Wake up!' I hissed urgently. 'I think there's another Oldway Creature coming. And it's flying!'

'Rubbish,' he said. 'Oldways can't fly. You're imagining things, Tanz. Or dreaming.' And he went back to sleep.

I looked up. The stars were almost completely obscured now. T.A. was wide awake beside me.

'I don't know what it is, Tanz,' she said, shakily, 'but it's horribly big!'

'If you can see it too, I'm not dreaming.' I grabbed Gwydion by the hair and tugged at it until he woke up.

'Ow! Stop it! What do you think you're doing?'

'Gwydion,' I pleaded. 'Look up?'

At last he sat up and looked, rubbing the sleep out of his eyes. 'Oh, no need to worry about that,' he said, when he had focused on the huge shape hovering above us. 'It's only Bugsy.' He lay down again and closed his eyes.

I prodded him. 'What do you mean, it's only Bugsy?'

'Bugsy. My dragon. I had him when I was about ten. Had to let him go just before Merlin turned me into your cat. Got too big to keep in the house. Kept knocking down walls and setting fire to things.'

I looked up. Now that he mentioned it, I could see that the thing was vaguely dragon-shaped. I remembered the great red beast that had guarded Castell y Ddraig and Gwydion's father before Gwydion had become Dragonking in his place, and wondered if it was the same dragon. No wonder Gwydion wasn't worried. This dragon was sort of a household pet. It felt comforting to have it about, and its great wings made a cooling breeze as it circled for a while, looking down on us, then flew over the rim of the hollow and away.

I don't know why people have difficulty believing in dragons. Everybody believes in Tyrranosaurus Rex and Diplodocus, right? So what's so hard to believe about a dragon?

Once Bugsy (weird name, right? I must remember to ask Gwydion about that one day) had flown away, T.A and I settled down to sleep. And despite the variety of snores – five Oldway Creatures, two wolfhounds, Gwydion, Taliesin, O'Liam and assorted men-at-arms – I slept quite well, thank you!

17

There was a sense of great excitement in the camp next day: a sort of 'at last we're doing something' sort of feeling. The Oldways were sitting in a well-behaved, tidy line watching men-at-arms scuttle around giving each other orders, polishing shields and rubbing greasy stuff into leather armour, sharpening swords and swinging them energetically around their heads with fierce expressions on their faces.

Gwydion's expression was grumpy. 'I tell you I'm perfectly fit and well, Nest!' he said crossly. 'There's nothing wrong with me but a bit of a scratch and a sore leg. I can fight just as well as anyone.'

'Rubbish,' Taliesin said. 'If you come with us, you might get killed this time. Is that what you want? You can't hold a sword properly. You can't even stand up for any length of time.'

'I tell you I'm well enough. This is my country, and I'm going to fight for it.'

'No you aren't, Gwydion,' Nest said. 'Flissy?'

They got one each side of him. Taliesin tripped him up and caught him, Flissy held his nose until he opened his mouth, and Nest poured some medicine down his throat, then held his mouth shut so he couldn't spit it out. I seemed to remember doing the same for Fflur, my wolfhound, with worm tablets once, with much the same result. As soon as he was released, Gwydion growled and snapped and shook his head and coughed.

And fell asleep. Taliesin lowered him gently to his mattress.

'There,' Flissy rubbed her hands together in satisfaction. 'There's more than one way of getting a man to do as he's told besides talking him to death, right, Nest? And that stuff will keep him asleep for a good twenty-four hours. Unless we give him the antidote to wake him up.'

Iestyn, trotted over, buckling his sword around his waist and looking very serious. 'Taliesin, will you command the soldiers? I'll take on the command of the villagers, and the Lady, of course, will be in charge of everything else.'

Oh. Right. I tried to look enthusiastic, and committed, and as if I knew what sort of a plan would be really good.

'I think,' Taliesin said carefully, seeing my expression, 'that we should have a meeting before we attack. To be absolutely honest, I don't think the Lady is quite certain that attacking in broad daylight is a good idea. Right, Tan'ith?'

'Oh, absolutely,' I said, nodding vigorously. 'Night would be much better. Quieter. More people asleep. Darker.' And much, much farther away than right now, my cowardy-bits thought.

O'Liam was bouncing at my elbow. 'I don't care what time we attack them no good spalpeens!' he spluttered. 'Just let me at them. Wasn't they after shutting me up in a dark dungeon with nothing to eat at all at all, and me starving to death the whole terrible while?'

'I suggest we all get some breakfast,' Flissy said, 'and then we can make our plans to attack Castell y Ddraig.'

So we ate, and then the Council of War, including Iestyn, O'Liam and Eifion Gwyn as Iestyn's deputy, settled down under our pow-wow tree to discuss what, exactly, we would be doing. I leaned my back against the tree and looked around. A glint of shining russet caught my eye, poking out from behind a tent. I knew exactly who that was.

'Branwen?' I called. 'Don't hide yourself away. Come and sit beside me.'

Shyly the little girl emerged from her hiding place. 'I daren't, Lady,' she said, blushing scarlet. She picked up the end of her plait and munched it. 'Our Dada will be furious with me!' She eyed her father nervously.

'She don't have no place here, Lady,' Eifion Gwyn said, nodding furiously. 'She'm just a useless, silly girl with spotty dapples and red hair.'

'As I was, not so very long ago,' I said frostily. 'And since it was Branwen that saved everybody's lives, including the Dragonking's, when the castle was attacked, I think she deserves to sit in on our discussion.' I thought 'so there!' but I didn't say it. I could already see Taliesin smirking at the spotty dapples bit, and T.A. was having a bit of a grin, too. Eifion Gwyn's trouble was that he hadn't heard of Women's Rights, and he had a lot of trouble with women being Assertive. Especially me. However, if I could get his daughter used to sticking up for herself I could ensure him a fairly miserable time. I hoped!

Branwen sidled over, keeping plenty of space between herself and her furious father, who subsided into a muttery heap. She sat beside me and I put my arm round her and gave her a hug. 'Don't let anyone ever tell you that you are "just a useless girl", Branwen.' I told her firmly. 'Girls can do anything boys can do, and usually quieter, better, and with less mess. Right?'

She didn't say anything, but she nodded furiously, blushing with delight.

And so we laid our plans.

At midnight, our determined army slipped out of the mountain hideout. As well as the men-at-arms, a lot of the women came with us, and from the expressions on their faces, heaven help any baddie who got in their way.

Most of the men had horses, and some took the women pillion behind or in front of them. Taliesin, Nest, T.A., O'Liam and I shifted into owls and flew low above the riders as they urged their mounts down the silent mountainside, across the valley and up the lower slopes of the next peak. The Oldway Creatures lolloped along at the rear, so that they wouldn't spook the horses. Just below the summit everyone waited, while Taliesin and I soared over the escarpment and down a little way to where the great bulk of Castell y Ddraig loomed, a darker shadow against the darkness of the mountainside.

A few lights glimmered through arrowslits, and there was the sound of the scrape of metal on stone as the watchmen paced the battlements. Our battlements. Taliesin and I circled the walls once, twice. On each of the four sides there was a watchman. Each man patrolled his quarter of the castle: up, down, up, down. At least, three of them did. On one side, the watchman was fast asleep, leaning against the wall, with his mouth open. He smelled rather strongly of ale, and if his sergeant-major had spotted him, he'd have been for the high jump – probably right off the battlements. And to make matters even worse – for their side at least – his patrol was right over the main gate of the castle…

Hovering above him, I nodded to Taliesin. He flew back to the others to tell them where we would attack, and I flew silently over the castle walls and down into the courtyard. It was as messy as ever, in fact possibly more so, because there was more rubbish piled everywhere, and it smelled as if – well, I won't go into details. You might be reading this as you're eating your dinner, after all.

I flew into the gateway. The great bronze portcullis loomed overhead, open, and only the heavy wooden doors stood closed against us. I flew into the shadows, shifted back, and, once I was comfortable in my skin, moved forward into the dim moonlight and put my hands on the great wooden bar that lay across the slots in the door, barring it from the inside. I'd just begun to lift when a door opened about half-a-metre away, flooding the gateway – and me – with candlelight, and a man appeared.

'Hey! What do you think you're doing, you? C'mere!' He was large and overweight, which is probably why he missed me when he made a grab. I darted away, and zapped him with a quick spell. My aim wasn't very good, getting caught unaware like that, but it bounced off the wall, ricocheted, and hit him right between the eyes. They crossed, and he slid down the wall with a happy smile on his face. He took no further interest in me or the gate at all.

I sidled over to the open door and looked inside the

guardroom. There were three men in there, playing cards and glugging down something that probably wasn't Tŷ Nant spring water, from the red noses and bleary faces. It was a second's work to chuck a spell to land in the middle of the table and spatter each of them with sleepy-drops. And then the way was clear for me to open the castle gate.

The bar was heavy, and I had to struggle to shove it up and out, but as soon as it slid sideways onto the cobblestones, I grabbed the huge ring handles, opened the latch and swung both doors open. Once I was outside, I waved frantically to the waiting army of men-at-arms and villagers.

They came silently down – well, as silently as a lot of large, clumsy blokes on horses can manage, anyhow – and filtered into the castle. When everyone was inside, Taliesin and I closed the heavy doors again, but didn't drop the bar down – we needed to keep our escape route free, after all.

It was a short battle, and fairly bloodless, because everyone except three watchmen was fast asleep, and nobody seemed very interested in fighting when they woke up and found a sharp sword poised beneath their left nostril! Even though they were all foreigners – there were some Germans, some dark-skinned swarthy-looking men who spoke a language I couldn't identify, a couple of Frenchmen and a great number of English – they soon got the general idea that we wanted them to get out of bed, quick, and behave themselves rather well. The men-at-arms and villagers rounded them all up and herded them into the castle courtyard, where we set the Oldway Creatures to surround them, menacingly, and guard them. Our men stood outside the circle and kept an eye open for anyone who looked likely to try to sneak off. Not that anyone would, probably. It would take a braver man than any of them to try to wriggle past an Oldway!

Taliesin, T.A., Nest, Eifion Gwyn, Iestyn, and a couple of men-at-arms and I went looking for Rhiryd Goch and his brothers Ardwyn, and of course, Jason of the Golden Fleas. Ardwyn and Jason we found quickly enough, and the men-at-arms prodded them downstairs at sword-point to join the others. They were bickering all the way down the spiral staircase about whose fault it was that they'd been captured.

Rhiryd ap Rhiryd Goch slept foxily in what had once been Gwydion's father's great bed: a four-poster hung with white curtains richly embroidered with crimson dragons and golden crowns. I was quite glad Gwyd wasn't there to see him snoring, scruffy and unwashed between the silk sheets.

Taliesin moved silently to the bedside, and poked the sleeping figure with the sharp end of his sword. Rhiryd grunted, and opened one eye. Then the other one snapped open, and he sat up, opening his mouth to bellow. Then he closed it again.

'Quite right, too,' I said, approvingly. 'You could shout all you like, but no one would come. They're all nicely parcelled up in the courtyard. We're about to ask them to leave. We rather thought you'd like to join them. Not, of course, that we are going to let *you* go.'

I wondered what we were going to do with them, but I was quite sure that Taliesin had something in mind. I hoped it wouldn't be too painful, or too bloody. Just permanent, that's all. I was fed up with people upsetting Ynys Haf and sticking swords and spears and stuff into my Gwydion. It's just that, being a goodwitch, you can't get too bloodthirsty. It just isn't expected of one, is it?

Anyway, the three brothers were separated from their men, and kept aside. Taliesin, who has a gift for languages (well, he used to be a teacher, didn't he? Teachers are expected to know stuff like that. Even if he was a music teacher.) explained to the mercenary soldiers that they had three choices. One, they could carry on trying to fight us – and the Oldway Creatures; two, they could leave their swords and stuff in a nice, tidy pile and get permanently lost. Out of Ynys Haf, right away, for good, and never darken our doorstep again, sort of thing. Or, three, they could get turned into something small, slimy, short-lived and fairly brainless, that inhabited the (usually fertile) soil of Ynys Haf. A worm, say. Or a slug.

The mercenaries looked at each other, and muttered in various languages. Some of them waved their arms about a lot. Then from about their persons they produced a large collection of pocket knives, small daggers, slingshots, pebbles, knuckle-dusters and other instruments usually used to inflict grievous bodily harm on someone else, and tossed them into a neat pile in the middle of the courtyard. Then, escorted by five large Oldways nudging them along in quite a friendly manner for Oldways, they broke all land speed records getting out of the main gate and heading for the coast. The fishing fleet would make a fortune shipping this lot out.

That left Rhiryd ap Rhiryd, Jason and Ardwyn. The twins shuffled their feet and looked nervously at each other. Ardwyn sniffled, and wiped his nose on his sleeve. Jason carefully stepped behind him, keeping his brother's body in between himself and Taliesin and me. He didn't know that the Oldways had come lolloping back, and were standing right behind him.

'Right,' I said. 'What AM I to do with you three? I thought I'd actually got rid of you last time we tangled, but here you are again, poking your noses in where they aren't wanted.'

'And shutting me up in a dungeon, entirely, so they did!' O'Liam said indignantly at my elbow.

'You really don't know where you aren't welcome, do you?' I went on. 'I don't care if your father did have delusions of grandeur and think he could rule Ynys Haf in Gwydion Dragonking's place. He was wrong. He was stupid, and you three are even stupider.'

'And they didn't give me anything at all to eat, at all!' O'Liam reminded me.

'And you captured my friend here, and locked him up and starved him,' I said, to shut O'Liam up, who was distracting me.

'And they chained me up with great shackles, and with not even the decency to use iron that I could form some type of good relationship with, either,' O'Liam muttered.

'We should have killed you,' Rhiryd ap Rhiryd snarled, 'while we had the chance.'

'Ooh! Did you not hear that, Lady?'

'I did, O'Liam.'

'Will you punish them for that, Lady?'

'I will, O'Liam.'

'Can I watch, Lady?'

'You can, O'Liam.'

Ardwyn and Jason made wonderful slugs. And the sun was coming up in the East, waking up the birds, and from the way they were peering hungrily from various ledges and battlements all over the castle, I didn't give much for Ardwyn and Jason's chances of living to see sunset. I bent down over the slugs. 'If you want to survive, you two, I'd learn how to run, if I were you!'

The slugs looked at each other, and started to slither…

'As for you –' I turned to Rhiryd ap Rhiryd. 'You are staying here. Gwydion Dragonking would like a word with you. Several words, actually.'

Rhiryd ap Rhiryd Goch was introduced, to O'Liam's great satisfaction, to the dungeon that the leprechaun had formerly occupied and shackled to the very same wall, but with strong iron shackles. The villagers headed back to the safe place in the mountains to fetch their children and take them home, and the men-at-arms set about making the castle habitable again, with lots of buckets of water from the well (which thankfully hadn't been affected by the drought). Soon the courtyard echoed with cries of disgust at the mess that had been left behind.

Taliesin and Iestyn went to fetch Gwydion, and T.A. and I found a clean-ish corner in one of the chambers. I magicked us some sleeping bags, and we went to sleep.

When I woke up, T.A.'s sleeping bag was empty.

18

At first I didn't worry. In fact, I turned over and went back to sleep for a while. When I finally woke up and went looking for her, though, no one had seen her since the night before, and no one knew where she was. *Then* I started to worry.

I went looking for Taliesin, who was sitting in the solar, writing with a quill pen on a parchment. He shook the pen irritably. 'What I wouldn't give for a decent biro,' he grumbled. 'Or a rollerball. Even a pencil. I'd bring one through a Time Door if I thought I could get it past Merlin. But you know what he's like.'

'Never mind that, I can't find T.A.,' I said, worriedly.

'What do you mean, you can't find her? Drat!' he said, mopping up a huge blot with a shaker of sand.

'When I woke up this morning her sleeping bag was empty, and no one has seen her.'

'Well, perhaps she's wandered off for a walk or something. Leave it for a while. I'm sure she'll be back.'

For once he was wrong. By the time the sun was high overhead, beating down in a cloudless sky (it was so hot in the sun-trap courtyard it was like being hit on the head with a hammer) there was still no sign of her. By that time, Gwydion, who was like a bear with a sore head because we had tricked him the night before, had arrived.

'Where can she have gone?' I worried, chewing at my lower lip. 'This isn't like her. You don't suppose…'

‘What?’ Nest asked.

‘Oh, I don’t know. I can’t think of anything we should really be worried about. After all, we’ve got Maebh and Rhiryd ap Rhiryd, and Ardwyn and Jason are slugs, right? So who’s left to worry about?’

Flissy frowned. ‘Perhaps she’s wandered off and got lost,’ she suggested. ‘She doesn’t know Ynys Haf as well as we do, after all. Nest, why don’t you get out the scrying bowl and have a look?’

But just as she was about to fill the bowl with water, a man-at-arms clattered up the stairs and crashed through the door. He was carrying an arrow with gaudy purple flights. There was a piece of paper tied round the shaft.

‘This just came in over the wall, Sire,’ he said waving it at Gwydion. ‘It just missed my butty Twp Dai by *that* much, Sire! Dangerous, that is. Twp Dai have come over all unnecessary with the shock. Don’t know why folks can’t use the Royal Pigeon instead of doing daft things like that with sharp arrows and stuff!’

Gwydion took the arrow and unwrapped the note. Everyone craned their necks to see over his shoulder.

‘Oh, crumbs,’ I said, miserably. ‘She’s gone and done it now!’

Dragonking, it began,

I have captured the mortal. You have Rhiryd ap Rhiryd and The Princess Maebh. If you will give me your prisoners, I will give you mine.

Otherwise, she dies.

It was signed (with a lot of squiggly, show-off type flourishes)

Master Theophilus Henbane

'Theophilus!' Taliesin said. 'No wonder he turned out bad.'

'This is no time for jokes,' Gwydion muttered. 'T.A. needs us. What can we do?'

'We could do what he asks,' I suggested. 'Let Maebh and ap Rhiryd go. And then we'd have T.A. back.'

'Even if we did that, which we couldn't possibly, given the circumstances, Tanz, you don't honestly think he'd let her go, do you?' Gwydion said bitterly. 'Of course he won't. He'll wait until he has Maebh and ap Rhiryd, and then he'll still keep her. We have to find her and rescue her. We can't even think of doing a deal with someone like Henbane. All we have to do is find him.'

'How? He's invisible,' I reminded him.

'And whose fault is that?' Taliesin reminded me.

'All right, all right, it's mine. How was I to know that he hadn't vanished completely? Anyway, it's done now. It's too late. But T.A. isn't invisible, so wherever T.A. is, he will be there too, right? Think, everybody, *think*. How can we find T.A.?'

'I could try scrying,' Nest suggested, 'but I have a feeling he'll have shielded her somehow so that I can't pick up her aura.'

'Oh, rats,' I said miserably. 'The only thing we can possibly do is just – start looking.'

'Well, he's not going to be far away, is he?' Gwydion said. 'He just shot an arrow over the battlements: he couldn't do that from too far away.'

'You're right,' Taliesin agreed. 'But don't forget he's invisible.'

'Oh. Yes.'

'Hang on a minute!' I waved my arms. 'He's

invisible – but his bow isn't! And where there's an arrow, there has to be a bow, right?'

'Right!'

'So all we have to do is find a bow travelling by itself, right?'

'Except he's probably dumped it somewhere,' Flissy said, and I sagged again.

'Would you mind if I said a word or two now?' O'Liam put in.

I sighed. 'Go on, O'Liam. What?'

'Well,' he said, his pointed golden face bright with enthusiasm, 'Master Theophilus Henbane might be invisible, so.'

We nodded. There was no arguing with that.

'But do you not recall the smelly stuff he would plaster on his hair to stick it down and make it shiny?'

We nodded. It stank of violets.

'And outside in the courtyard, do we not have the finest set of tracking beasts in the whole country?'

'What, Bran and Garan?' Taliesin said doubtfully. 'They're good, but –'

'No, you eejit!' O'Liam bounced up and down excitedly. 'The great beastie things! The Oldway Creatures! Don't they have noses on their faces like great chimbleys?'

'They do,' Taliesin agreed, 'but how will they know what scent to follow?'

'Well,' O'Liam pointed out, 'when he lived in Castell Du, did he not leave his belongings behind? After all, he was in no position to pack his stuff before he left, was he, now?'

We all looked hopefully at each other. 'Fliss, do you remember if he left stuff behind?' I asked.

She thought. 'He did, I'm sure of it! I think one of the chambermaids stuffed it in a pillowcase. It must be there somewhere. Come on!'

We all shifted into starlings and flocked out the window. Within an hour we were flying in over the battlements of Castell Du. We shifted back to ourselves in the deserted, filthy courtyard. Gwydion looked around him. 'Just look at the state of this place,' he said angrily. 'It will take weeks of work to get it back to what it was.'

'Not if we magic the worst away,' I suggested. 'But never mind that now, Gwydion. Everybody. Start looking. We've got no time to waste.'

We tried the chambermaids' quarters first: we discovered a lot of hair-ribbons, some love-letters and a very trashy manuscript which no respectable young chambermaid should have been reading anyway, but none of Henbane's belongings.

We tried the store-rooms, but apart from empty food containers and a rat (which I got rid of very quickly) there was nothing there, either.

'If there's anything belonging to him here,' I said, 'then it will still be in one of the bedchambers. Come on, let's take one each. We have to find something, anything, that belonged to Henbane.'

It was O'Liam who found it. I heard the little man shriek with excitement. When we rushed into the room he was searching, he was hopping up and down, waving a pillowcase. 'Will you zbell de awful zbell on this ding?' he said, holding his nose. 'It zdingks! It sdingks of Theophilus Hedbade!'

It did. It was a sweet, sickly, horrible smell that instantly reminded me of the nasty, oily, greasy person who went with it. Taliesin volunteered to carry it back in his beak – he wasn't a starling this time but a buzzard. He was looking a decidedly greenish buzzard by the time he landed at Castell y Ddraig and shifted back. He spat the pillow-case out and pulled a face. 'Oh, that was disgusting! Ugh! Someone get me a drink of something, please!'

I magicked him an orange juice, and he drank it down. 'Thanks,' he said. That's much better. Now. Where are those creatures?'

Not than anyone could miss them. It was what's known as a rhetorical question. You can't exactly miss five very large monsters lying in a sleepy, affectionate heap in the middle of the courtyard, can you?

We woke them up, and they loomed dopily over us.

'Hang on a minute,' I said, 'we can't just send them off, can we? We won't be able to keep an eye on them. We have to go with them.'

'What do you suggest?' Nest asked, 'shift and follow?'

'No. We'll ride them!'

Taliesin looked dubious and O'Liam tried to disappear.

'Oh, come on! It'll be fun! And after all, they aren't dangerous any more.'

'Not until you fall off them, they aren't,' Taliesin muttered.

'What about me? I'm fed up with getting left behind all the time.'

'Oh, Gwydion, you couldn't possibly ride a creature! Your leg would probably drop off or something.'

He scowled. Then his face brightened. 'No, you're right. I couldn't ride. But there's nothing wrong with my arms. I'm going to shift and fly with you. There's no way you lot are leaving me behind again.'

We couldn't talk him out of it, and he certainly wouldn't fall for the 'trip-him-up-and-pour-the-potion' trick again.

So Taliesin, Nest, Flissy, and a very reluctant O'Liam and I each rode one of the beasts while Gwydion shifted into a sharp-eyed peregrine falcon and flew above us.

'If your arms get tired or your side hurts, Gwyd,' I reminded him, 'you can always hitch a ride on an Oldway Creature's head, right?' He flexed his dark blue, scimitar-shaped wings and nodded. Then he bent his knees and launched himself up into the air, hovering above us while Taliesin gave each of the Creatures – and Bran and Garan, for good measure – a good, long sniff of the pillowcase. The wolfhounds sneezed and backed away, but the Creatures looked quite interested.

'Now, *seek!*' I wasn't sure if they understood me, but they got the general idea. They gathered their muscles underneath themselves and lumbered off in pursuit of the pillowcase's smell, bending their long necks to sniff the ground every few yards or so. For a while they cast in circles, sniffing, and making a peculiar groaning sound deep in their throats, as if they were talking to one another. And then the biggest one, the one with the two horns, the one I was riding, unfortunately, suddenly let out a yodelling noise, like one of those Swiss blokes on a mountain-top, and set off at a gallop in the general direction of where Cricieth would be in about a thousand years' time.

I can't honestly say it was a comfortable ride: I spent most of it hanging on to my creature's horns for dear life. The trouble was, of course, that I didn't have a saddle, and riding a scaly neck without a saddle gets a bit painful after a time, even if a person is wearing leather trousers. Hot leather trousers. By the time the five creatures skidded to a halt on the edge of a wood, I felt as if there wasn't a square centimetre of skin left on the inside of my legs at all.

All the Creatures, and Bran and Garan, were craning their necks – 'pointing' towards a path that led into a deep, dark forest. And despite the bright, almost unbearably hot sun, the forest was decidedly sinister.

But there was nothing else for it, was there? If T.A. was in there somewhere, we had to go in and find her, right?

Right.

19

At first, the forest wasn't too scary. We dismounted from our beasts because of the danger of colliding with overhanging branches, and left the Oldway Creatures flopped in a heap on the outskirts. We just took Bran and Garan in with us.

The sun dropped bright, wavery coins of light in our paths where it filtered through the canopy of leaves, but then as we went deeper the trees grew thicker, and all the light we had was a dim, woody green-ness. It should have been cooler in the forest, but instead it was as if all the heat of the day was trapped in there: all that was missing was the direct beat of the sun on top of our heads.

Normally, the wolfhounds would have bounded on ahead of us, shoving their heads down rabbit-holes, investigating bushes and pushing their noses along the ground after delicious smells. This time they hung back, so that they were close beside us, and Garan growled nervously at the sudden crack of a twig or sway of a branch. There was something they didn't like about this particular forest. And that made three of us.

Taliesin was in the lead, following a faint path through the trees; Gwydion next, then Nest, Flissy, O'Liam and me. Bran was in front with Taliesin, Garan stayed in the rear with me, and I was glad of his company. There was a feeling of wrongness about this forest, a feeling of something-lurking-waiting-to-pounce. And I never forgot for one second that the person we were hunting was invisible.

We went deeper and deeper into the wood. Fallen trees blocked the path and we had to climb over them; termites and huge wood ants scuttled away from us as we searched. The trees themselves seemed to lean towards us, stretching out long, gnarled branches that tapped our shoulders as we passed them, and flicked our faces with stinging twigs. If someone had jumped out from behind a tree and said 'Boo!' all six of us, and the wolfhounds as well, would probably have fainted.

Then, as I stepped over a tree-trunk, I had this horrible feeling that I'd stepped over it before. There was a knot of sickly orange fungus growing on the side of it that looked vaguely familiar, and I began to wonder if we were actually going anywhere, or if we were walking round in circles.

The thought must have hit Taliesin at about the same time, because he paused, and looked around us. 'We've been here before,' he said. 'This path is doubling back on us.'

'Don't you mean we're doubling back on the path?' Flissy said, but he shook his head. 'No. It's the path. Someone has fixed it, somehow. Does anyone else feel it?'

'Me,' I said. 'I was just thinking the exact same thing. We'll never find T.A. if the forest won't let us.'

'Yes, we will.' Nest put out her hand and touched my arm. 'If there's an enchantment on a forest, then if you know about it, you can take it off. Remember, you are the Lady of Ynys Haf.'

'I'm not doing much of a job at it though, am I?'

'Yes you are.' Taliesin put his arm round me. 'Come

on, Tanz. You just need to concentrate. Feel the forest. Let it talk to you.'

So I concentrated. After a while I felt the forest flood into me, felt its pathways snaking round and crossing, doubling back when we weren't looking. And I felt, underneath, the unhappiness of the forest because something was making it act like that. It was easy after that. I just felt my way to the root of the problem, found the knot that was causing the paths to tangle, and untied it. All in my head, of course. The forest instantly felt better. The air was cooler, and occasional fragments of sunlight broke through the gloom.

'There,' Taliesin said. 'Come on. I knew you could do it, Tanz!'

We set off again, this time walking with more confidence, although I noticed that Bran and Garan still stayed close to us, and wondered who was protecting who!

Suddenly, Taliesin stopped, Gwydion bumped into him, and the rest of us slowed down.

'Listen,' Taliesin's tanned face looked pale in the dim light, and O'Liam was tinted as green by the tree-light as I'd once imagined a leprechaun would be.

'What?' I hissed back. 'I can't hear anything.'

'Then shut up and *listen*,' Taliesin said.

I still couldn't hear anything, and then – I started to grin. Somewhere, still quite a way off, someone was singing.

'We all live in a yellow submarine, yellow submarine, yellow submarine,

We all live in a yellow submarine, yellow submarine, submarine.'

'T.A.! It's got to be!' At least, I couldn't think of anyone else in Ynys Haf likely to be singing ancient Beatles songs! Once she'd finished 'Yellow Submarine', she went on to 'Ten Green Bottles', and then she started on all the Girl Guide songs we'd ever learned. She was on verse two of 'We are the Red Men, tall and quaint', her voice getting louder as we got closer to her, when we found her.

She was in a strange sort of clearing in the wood. In the middle of it was a large, hollow cairn of stones, and inside the cairn was my friend, tied up very tightly with strong ropes. She had once been gagged, as well, but she'd managed to wriggle the gag down over her chin, which was why she'd been able to sing.

'Thank goodness,' she sighed, 'I was beginning to run out of songs. The only ones I could think of were rude rugby ones, and I didn't want to start on those.'

We untied her. The gag was a green-spotted purple handkerchief, and it stank of Henbane's violet hair oil. 'Pooh!' I said, chucking it in a corner.

'You ought to try having it stuffed in your mouth, Tanz,' T.A. said feelingly.

'Where's Henbane?' Taliesin asked.

T.A. shrugged. 'He went off somewhere. Not that you can actually tell where he is, him being invisible, of course. I'd rather like to get out of here before he comes back, if it's all the same to you.'

'He IS back,' a silky voice said, somewhere behind us. 'And no one is going anywhere. I knew you'd try to get the mortal back. How foolish of you.' A glowing ball of hideous greenish light appeared in mid air and hurtled towards us.

'Duck!' I hollered, and luckily, everyone did. I hurled a spell back in the direction that the spell had come from, but of course Henbane wasn't there any more. Another spell came from a different direction, and five of us were whirling round like dervishes trying to anticipate where the next spell was coming from. The sixth of us, O'Liam, was trying to insert himself under a rock, and T.A., wisely, got as far back in the cairn's hollow heart as she could.

We ducked and dodged and hurled futile spells at an invisible enemy, getting more and more tired. Nest got caught by the fall-out from one of the spells and fell over in a faint, Flissy was panting and out of breath, Gwydion was pale, with perspiration pouring down his face with the exertion, and I was beginning to get desperate. Taliesin was chucking spells around as well, but because we couldn't see what we were aiming at, we didn't have a hope of hitting Henbane.

And then T.A., who had been keeping well out of everyone's way since she wasn't equipped in the spell department, suddenly leapt up from where she was crouched and ran over to me.

'Tanz!' she whispered. 'I think I know how to beat Henbane!'

'Then tell me about it,' I said, gritting my teeth and dodging a spell composed of white light, heat, and hornets. 'Quick!'

'*Give everyone a pot of paint!*' she whispered behind her hand.

'Paint? Oh, for goodness sake, T.A.! What a time to think about decorating!' I wasn't concentrating on what she was saying. I was too busy pushing her out of the way of a thunderbolt full of vipers.

'No, you dingbat! *Think!*'

And then my brain clicked into gear. In seconds everyone was equipped with a large, open pot of Dulux Apple White Matt – and thankfully everyone was quicker on the uptake than I was.

As soon as the next spell appeared in mid-air, we all threw our pots at the place it came from – and inevitably some splodges of the paint stuck to Henbane. He was invisible, but the paint wasn't, and at last we could see bits of him. Not a lot, but enough splodges of paint moving about in mid air to tell where he was – at last!

Taliesin, a large dollop of Apple White dripping off the end of his nose, grinned at me, and zapped Henbane with a serious spell. He dodged it, but Nest's hit him on the ankle. His right leg suddenly had a large ball and chain attached to it, and Gwydion finished the job with a rope that materialised at Henbane's ankles and wound itself tightly all the way up his body. In the end he had so much rope round him he looked like a badly-wrapped Egyptian mummy!

T.A. sauntered over and put her face very close to his. 'Apple White doesn't suit you at all,' she said. 'And if you EVER lay ONE FINGER on me again, I will pull out every hair on your greasy little head and stuff it right up your nose, understand?'

Henbane, the rope wound firmly round him, couldn't even nod. We couldn't see his eyes, they hadn't been caught in the sploshes of paint – but I bet they'd have been panic stricken if we could have seen them!

'We can't let him stay invisible, Taliesin,' Gwydion said. 'Once the paint has worn off we won't be able to see him. Can you undo the spell Tanith put on him?'

Naturally, he could. He scratched his head and thought a bit, and then muttered a couple of words under his breath. Henbane's outline blurred a bit, and then, slowly, all of him that was outside the ropes, became visible. I was right. His eyes WERE panic-stricken.

'Well, that's all sorted out,' Taliesin said. 'I think it's time I went back to Merlin. He's going to be rather annoyed with me anyway, because I've been away so long. He told me I had twenty-four hours, that's all, and I've been away much longer than that.'

'But –' I said, intending to mention the fact that I still had a bit of a problem and I could do with some help. Remember Conor of the Land Beneath, Taliesin? But it was too late. He took a deep breath, shut his eyes, held his nose, and jumped upward. He didn't come down again, thus disproving one of the oldest beliefs of mankind – that what goes up must come down. He just wasn't there any more.

'Oh, thanks a bunch,' I said crossly. 'Need any help, Tanz? Shall I sort out Conor for you, Tanz? That's typical, that is. Never here when he's needed.'

'Oh, shut up, Tanz,' Gwydion said. 'Taliesin knows perfectly well that you can cope. At least, you can cope now I'm up and about.'

'I could cope perfectly well without you, thank you very much!'

'Sure you could.'

Going back, the wood didn't seem quite as scary as

it had before. The Oldway Creatures were waiting patiently for us, and we tied Henbane onto one of their backs before shifting, like Gwydion, to peregrine falcons and heading for home, hovering above the Creatures' heads, the wolfhounds loping alongside them.

For all Gwydion's boasts, by the time we got back to Castell y Ddraig he was exhausted. He flopped onto the cobbles of the courtyard, and his shift back to his own shape seemed to take ages. Nest took one look at him and bustled him into his chamber to rest.

Master Henbane was accommodated in the next-door dungeon to Rhiryd ap Rhiryd Goch. We untied him, but I couldn't bring myself to put iron chains on someone who was magic: I knew what it felt like, and it was bad enough being locked up in a dungeon, let alone being made to feel horribly ill, as well. I'm just an old softie at heart, right? I contented myself with putting him in the dungeon with the biggest iron door. I gave him a wooden screen to hide behind, so the iron wouldn't get him, but I couldn't see any way he could magic himself out of there without approaching the iron door. I also put a force-field round the whole of the castle, above and below ground, so he couldn't get in the way I'd got into Castell Du, once. I let the guard slam the iron door behind him, left him standing outside with his pike just in case, and pootled happily off up the spiral stairs.

I felt good about things for once. OK, I still had to sort out the Conor problem, but I could cope with that. All I had to do was go to Conor, hand over Maebh, and talk him out of wanting O'Liam back. It might be a bit more difficult talking him into letting Siobhan Flowerface go as well – but I felt so confident I was sure I could do it.

Next I went and saw Maebh, who rolled up in a disgruntled ball when she saw me, her prickles sticking out. I felt a bit sorry for her, actually, because as a person she isn't the brightest bean around. It was Master Theophilus Henbane who had led her into trouble. Bad company and all that. So I magicked her a nice big bowl of Pedigree Chum, which hedgehogs adore, and some fresh water to drink.

'We've captured Henbane, Maebh,' I said. 'So it's all over, now. He can't do us any more harm, and neither can you.'

The hedgepig uncurled, and looked at me with its bright little eyes. The trouble is, I really like hedgepigs, and because that was the shape Maebh was in, I started to feel a bit sympathetic towards her. I was even thinking of opening her little wooden cage and letting her run about a bit, but then Flissy came in.

'What are you doing, Tanz?'

'Feeding Maebh. Do you think we could let her out for a while? Give her a chance to stretch her legs?'

'We could. But with Henbane so close, don't you think that's a bit of a risk? If you let her out and she got away and somehow found Henbane – well, he could change her back and then where would we be?'

'I suppose you're right. Sorry, Maebh. We can't trust you.'

'And besides, you have to take her back to Erin. You have a promise to keep to Conor of the Land Beneath, remember? Otherwise Ynys Haf will die from lack of water. And if Conor wants Maebh, and handing her over will save Ynys Haf, then Conor gets Maebh.'

When Aunty Fliss said this, I happened to be looking at Maebh. She suddenly became very still, and stared at me.

And two enormous tears formed in her bright, hedgepiggy little eyes and rolled down her face.

I felt *awful.*

20

So the next day, Gwydion, O'Liam, Maebh and I hopped on a boat at Gwyddno Garanhir's harbour and set off to Ireland. Maebh travelled in her string bag, O'Liam travelled almost as miserably as I did, and T.A. kicked up a huge fuss about not coming with us.

'You've got to take me!' she howled indignantly. 'The Ant said I had to be with you. It's me that's got to save you from some predicament you get yourself into!'

I patted her arm, soothingly, and she glared at me. 'You already did, T.A. You thought up the Dulux idea, right?'

'That might not be it,' she muttered sulkily. 'There might be some other terrible thing that you aren't expecting. You don't know, do you?'

'Look. From here on, it gets easier. All we have to do is go to Conor and talk to him. Gwydion will be with me, and he's Dragonking. Conor can't touch him, he's King of another country. From now it's just whatchamacallit – diplomacy, that's it.'

'You, diplomatic! Don't make me laugh!'

'No, not me. Gwydion. He's the diplomatic one.'

All I had to do was somehow find it in me to hand Maebh over to that nasty, sneaky, cruel little beast Conor. I had to. It was the only way to save Ynys Haf. Only I knew that if I did hand her over, I'd never forgive myself…

We had more sense than to land the boat at Big Deirdre's port: we put in on a wild, rocky bit of coastline a mile or two away, shifted into golden eagles and took turns to carry Maebh in her string bag because Gwydion still wasn't up to full strength.

Ireland undulated below us, great swathes of greenness stretching as far as the eye could see. It seemed strange to see long, silver ribbons of river twisting through lush valleys after the parched, dry yellowness of Ynys Haf.

Our strong wings beat the air, and we surfed on updraughts and plummeted down valleys. Once, O'Liam was almost overcome by the eagle in him and I had to stop him swooping down on a plump rabbit on the way. 'I'll feed you before we tackle Conor, I promise, O'Liam. But if you start eating raw rabbit at this stage you'll get terrible indigestion when I change you back to yourself, right?'

'If you say so, Lady. But that wee rabbit looked altogether like a fine snack, so it did.'

'Forget the bunny, O'Liam. Think chippety things with tomato sauce.'

Eventually, we came to the edge of the wood that hid the entrance to O'Liam's kingdom, and we flew to a mountain-top close by and perched on a crag. I changed, shifted O'Liam back, and Gwydion shimmered, stretched upward, and was himself again.

'Are you all right, Gwydion?' He didn't look all right. There were dark shadows under his eyes, and his normally dark skin was pale with tiredness.

'I'm fine. Only I don't think we'll tackle Conor tonight. I need some rest first.'

So we found a cave and rested for the night. O'Liam got his chippety things – he was getting so addicted to junk food I decided that once we got back to Ynys Haf I'd have to introduce him to some green vegetables whether he liked it or not – and Gwydion and I had steak pie with onions and gravy. Actually, so did O'Liam, when he'd finished his chips.

Gwydion slept like the dead, but I was wakeful and watchful, sleeping with one eye open for Big Deirdre, or anything else that might appear. In the early hours, I heard O'Liam get up and wander outside the cave. I followed him out.

'What's up?'

'Did I disturb you, Lady?'

'No. I was awake anyway. I'm a bit worried about Gwydion. I don't think he's properly fit yet, but he would come, wouldn't he.'

'Ah, he's a proper man, Lady. You should be proud of him, so.'

'I am, O'Liam. But what's the matter with you? Why can't you sleep?'

The leprechaun gave a big, gusty sigh. 'Oh, Lady. Here I am, back in Erin, and all of its music calls out to me to stay. But how can I? I'm sworn to the Dragonking, and my life wouldn't be worth a magic farthing if Conor got his hands on me. Not to mention the Bog Fairy and Big Deirdre. But this is my country, even as Ynys Haf is yours, and I long to stay here.'

'Will it be better if we can get Siobhan Flowerface away from here and back to Ynys Haf.'

'Oh, it will so. She's my sunshine, Lady, and will bring a bit of Erin with her when she comes. But did you not also promise I could visit my old Mammy before we left? Had you forgotten that?'

I had. 'I admit that your old Mammy had sort of

slipped my mind, O'Liam. Where does she live? Is she in the Land Beneath, or what?'

'She is so. She's Brigid of the Light Fingers, is my Mammy.'

Light fingers? Now, I don't know what 'light fingers' means to you, but to me it means someone who is a dab hand at acquiring other people's property. Nevertheless I gave him the benefit of the doubt. 'Good pastry-cook, is she, O'Liam?'

'She is not!' he said indignantly. 'Sure, and that's Mary Flourpaws' job! No,' he stuck out his chest and looked proud, 'my Mammy is the best thief in the whole Land Beneath, so she is. Can steal the food out of a man's mouth without him even dribbling, so she can!'

I made a mental note to keep a close eye on O'Liam's Mammy. Maybe thieves were more valued in the Land Beneath, among leprechauns, than they were in my Time among humans! Anyway, I promised O'Liam that we'd do our best to call in on his Mammy. He still looked worried, though.

'Is your man dead set on visiting Conor tomorrow, Lady?'

'Of course. Unfortunately, we have to. No choice, sort of thing.'

'Well, will you remember the saying we have in Erin?'

I sighed. 'What saying would that be, little chum?'

"An vair a bhíonn do lámh i mbéal an mhadra, tarraing go réidh i."

I was none the wiser. 'Which means?'

'When your hand is in the dog's mouth,' O'Liam said darkly, 'withdraw it gently.'

Thanks a bunch, O'Liam.

Gwydion looked better next morning, and after a good Welsh breakfast he looked better still. He wiped a runnel of egg-yolk off his chin and stood up. 'Right, let's get this show on the road.'

I picked up Maebh, who had curled in a miserable ball in her string bag. She hadn't touched the food I'd given her the night before, and she'd ignored her breakfast, too. 'I don't think it would be a good idea to take her with us, not at this point, anyway,' I decided. 'If we take her near Conor before we've reached any sort of an agreement, he might decide to grab her – and then we'd have nothing to bargain with.'

'The same could be said for me, also,' O'Liam said glumly. 'Sure, he's going to grab me and lock me up the very second he puts his eyes upon me, he is so.'

'No, he won't,' Gwydion patted the little man's shoulder. 'You're a free leprechaun now, by his own rules. You can decide what you are going to do with your own future, and at the moment at least you are part of my court. O'Liam Ironfinder, O'Liam of the Green Boots, First Leprechaun to the Court of the Dragonking of Ynys Haf!'

O'Liam's eyes went dreamy. 'Oh, it's a fine title to be sure, your honour, a fine title.'

'And besides, if you aren't with us, how are we going to recognise Siobhan and your Mammy?'

'That's true, so it is. And besides, you'll need me beside you. After all, I know Conor of the Land Beneath as well as anyone. And I know fine and well he is not to be trusted, he is not.'

We left Maebh in her string bag tucked away at the

back of the cave, a heavy stone on the edge of it so she couldn't run away, string bag and all.

I was inclined to agree with O'Liam about Conor. Nevertheless, we set off down the mountain. I was walking behind Gwydion, and I saw that, although he was still limping, he seemed better able to walk than he had been the day before. We were soon in the clearing in the woods where the opening to Conor's Land was. O'Liam was about to open the door in the tree, but Gwydion stopped him.

'I think perhaps we need to tidy ourselves a little bit before we meet Conor,' he suggested. 'After all, we've got standards to keep up!'

So, by the time O'Liam opened the door, we were all in our finest: Gwydion in the soft green leather waistcoat and trousers and pure white shirt he had worn at his crowning; me in a tawny silk dress with my Dragonqueen coronet, the emerald pendant and Arianrhod ring gleaming silver. O'Liam was decked out in emerald green satin with new, high-heeled matching boots (with flashing red lights in the heels – I couldn't resist it!) and a fine, cavalier-style hat with an enormous green feather in it.

He looked down at himself, and tapped his heels to make the lights flash. 'Sure and Siobhan will fall in love with me all over again, she will, when she sees me dressed so fine,' he sighed. 'With the little flashy lights in my boots and all. If only I didn't have to come face to face with Himself, mind, I'd be a happier leprechaun altogether, I would so.'

But nevertheless he opened the door, and we all trooped inside, O'Liam leading the way, then

Gwydion, then me. The leprechaun strutted importantly down the steep spiral stairs, along the corridors, until we came to the big doors of Conor's council chamber. Two leprechauns with a tall pikes stood in front of it, and when we approached they lowered the pikes, crossing them in front of us, barring our way.

'What? Do you bar Gwydion, Dragonking of Ynys Haf, from the presence of Conor of the Land Beneath?' O'Liam said haughtily (perhaps it was only me who noticed the little quiver of nervousness in his voice).

The pike-leprechauns looked at each other.

'Gwydion who?'

'Gwydion Dragonking. Of Ynys Haf,' O'Liam repeated.

'King, is he?'

'A great king,' O'Liam announced firmly.

'Where did you say he was from, then?'

'Ynys Haf,' O'Liam said, drawing himself up to his full height.

'Where might that be?'

'Across the Middlesome Sea.'

'Important, is he?'

'Oh, he is so.'

'Had we better let him in, Shaun?'

'Didn't his Lordship say he was not to be disturbed, Padraig? Not at all, at all, for anything?'

'But when his Lordship said that, was he knowing that Gwydion whatsisname was about to be visiting, Shaun?'

'He probably did not, Padraig.'

'Then what shall we do, Shaun?'

'I can't know that, Padraig.'

Gwydion got fed up with hanging about. He leaned forward over O'Liam's grand hat, and hissed, 'I am Gwydion, Dragonking of Ynys Haf, and this is the Lady of Ynys Haf. She is also a very powerful witch, and if you do not wish to spend the rest of your lives at the bottom of a pond going ribbit, ribbit, you will part those pikes and let us through. *Now*.'

Funnily enough, those pikes shot apart so fast that Padraig bashed himself on the nose with his, and made his eyes water. O'Liam turned the handle of the door and stood aside for Gwydion and me to sweep majestically in.

We may have looked majestic and stuff, but I was so nervous that I had a whole collection of butterflies having a butterfly ball in my middle.

Conor of the Land Beneath was having his fingernails polished by a fussy little leprechaun dressed all in purple satin. He glanced up as we entered, saw us and stood up suddenly, depositing the nail-polisher on his purple rear end.

'You!' he hissed, glaring at me. 'The leprechaun stealer. The promise-breaker. Have you come to keep your vow at last? Did you also bring Lady Haf, whom you took from me against her will? And who is this?'

O'Liam opened his mouth, but I raised my hand to shut him up. I had a feeling he was going to be grand again, and a grand O'Liam would certainly not go down well with Conor.

'My Lord Conor,' I said politely, 'may I introduce Gwydion, Dragonking of Ynys Haf.'

Gwydion inclined his head, but not too much. 'Cousin Conor.'

Conor looked up at Gwydion, his six foot, five inches almost touching the roof of his council chamber, and scowled. 'You are no cousin of mine, sir. You are too big. And your skin is an ugly colour.'

Gwydion wasn't rattled. 'We are cousins in our royal blood, Lord Conor. And although I may be much larger than you, and my skin a different colour, we are much alike. We are both extremely powerful in our own kingdoms, are we not?'

Conor sat down, tapping his fingers on the polished table. 'We are. Oh, we are indeed. But now, Gwydion Dragonking, you are in my kingdom. I have you, and your lady. And until your Lady keeps her promises, you are going nowhere at all.'

'Funny thing,' Gwydion said, sitting casually on the great, polished table, 'I thought you might say that!'

He was so cool! Trouble was, cool or not, I wasn't *quite* sure how he was going to get out of that one!

21

'I thought you might say that,' Gwydion said, 'but if you try to keep us here, not only will you incur the displeasure of Great Merlin, you will also never see Maebh again. So it depends, Conor of the Land Beneath, how much you want Maebh.'

Conor played with the fancy fringe on his coat. 'How can you promise me something that you do not have?'

'What, Maebh? Oh, we have Maebh. And once we have your assurance that I, the Lady, and O'Liam of the Green Boots may go as we came, unmolested, then you shall have her.'

'O'Liam of the Green Boots,' Conor sneered, glaring at the Leprechaun. 'A traitor, all decked out in his finery. We have a saying for it, do we not, O'Liam?'

'I imagine that we do, Lord Conor, I do so,' O'Liam said miserably.

'*Cuir síoda ar ghabhar agus is gabhar I geónaí é.*' Conor said. 'Put silk on a goat and it is still a goat.'

O'Liam went pale, and his mouth turned into a hard little line. Conor had blown any chance he had of getting O'Liam to stay behind willingly. And I knew that O'Liam was the only Ironfinder Conor had. He was more valuable than just about anyone else in Conor's kingdom, even if O'Liam himself did not know it.

Uninvited, Gwydion hooked a chair towards him and sat in it. He put his elbows on the table and stared hard at Conor. The leprechaun king glared back.

'So,' Gwydion said pleasantly. 'How shall we

handle this, Lord Conor? Shall I tell you what we want, and you will tell me what you want, and we shall see if, somewhere in the middle, we can agree?'

Sulkily, Conor of the Land Beneath nodded.

'Will you begin?' Gwydion leaned back, comfortably. He looked so laid back that I thought he might fall asleep.

'I want Maebh, of course. Your Lady –' he spat that out, scowling at me, '– your Lady promised I should have her. Immortal, as am I, but without her magic. That is my first demand.'

'And?'

'I want the Ironfinder back.'

'Is there anything else?'

'I want the Lady Haf. You stole her from me. I would have made her my Queen.'

In a pig's eye he would.

Gwydion nodded. 'Maebh you shall have,' he agreed. 'But O'Liam, by your own laws, has been away from your land for three full moons and three full days, and he is a free leprechaun. You may ask him if he wishes to stay. If he will not, then you may not ask for him.'

Conor glared at O'Liam. 'You will come back, Ironfinder. Now.'

O'Liam shook his head, nervously. 'No, your honour, I will not.'

'You betray your own people?'

'I do not! But I am sworn to the Dragonking, and I will not leave his side while he needs me.'

'A leprechaun's oath is worth nothing,' Conor sneered. 'There is always a way around a promise.'

'However –' Gwydion broke in, and O'Liam and Conor shifted their gaze to him.

'O'Liam is anxious that Siobhan Flowerface be allowed to leave with him.'

Conor smirked triumphantly. 'Never! She stays. You go. I have no use for traitors.'

O'Liam's shoulders sagged miserably.

'But,' Gwydion raised a finger. 'You need iron in the Land Beneath, Conor. Suppose O'Liam could be persuaded to return to your service – as a free leprechaun, mind, not as a bond-leprechaun as he was before – for one month each year. In that month he would find enough iron to last you the other eleven. Would you then allow him to have Siobhan Flowerface?'

Conor thought about it. 'One month?'

'One month. And he comes and goes as he wishes. You must do nothing to stop him or punish him. And in return he takes Siobhan Flowerface. Agreed?'

I rather wanted to point out that Gwydion hadn't actually asked O'Liam how he felt about it, but one look at O'Liam's face told me he was prepared to risk anything, put up with anything – even one month every year in Conor's clutches – to rescue Siobhan.

Conor tilted his chin and studied the polished roots that made up the ceiling of his council chamber. After a while, he said, 'Agreed. One month.'

'Now,' Gwydion went on. 'Your other request is to have the Lady Haf returned to you.'

Conor leaned forward, his eyes glinting.

'But since you held Lady Haf against her will, and

placed her under an enchantment, you have no claim to her.'

'But the Lady Haf loves me,' Conor said quickly. 'Has she not told you so?'

'Oh, she did,' I agreed. 'But once O'Liam took the enchantment off her, she didn't seem quite so keen, Conor. She went off you a bit. I think her actual words were, "what, love Conor of the Land Beneath? I'd rather poke myself in the eye with a sharp stick".'

'Thanks, Tanz,' Gwydion muttered under his breath. 'Shut up, will you?'

I shut up. Obviously, tact and diplomacy wasn't my big thing.

Conor's pointed golden face was a pattern of fury: his teeth were clenched and I'll swear his eyes glowed red in their sockets. Then he took a deep breath. 'But if the Lady Haf can be persuaded to return to me,' he said, 'and she wishes to stay, then there would be nothing at all you could do about that, would there?'

An expression of confusion flashed across Gwydion's face. 'No,' he agreed, after a while.

Conor's face relaxed into a knowing smile, which was about the time my antenna started to quiver with suspicion. 'Then I think we can reach agreement. I shall have Maebh, when you give her to me. I have the Ironfinder once a year for one month. And if the Lady Haf wishes to return to me of her own free will, then she may.'

And if you could look out of a window, Conor, I thought, *you might see a whole herd of pigs flying past!* What, T.A. have anything at all to do with Conor? Fat chance.

'So,' Conor went on, 'you agree?'

Gwydion considered, and then said, 'Agreed.'

'And now,' the leprechaun King said, 'what are your requests?'

'In return,' Gwydion said, leaning forward, so that he was eyeball to eyeball with Conor, 'I want whatever enchantment you have placed on Ynys Haf to be removed. At once. I want Siobhan Flowerface, free and without any strings attached, for O'Liam; I want O'Liam to be allowed to visit his mother before we leave, and afterwards his mother is to be treated with all honour. And lastly, I want all of us to be allowed to leave the Land Beneath without being troubled in any way.'

Conor leaned back, steepled his fingers and smiled. 'Agreed,' he said. 'And now, will you stay to dine with me?'

Trouble was, he'd agreed too quickly. And also, I didn't particularly like that smile. There was something about it that said 'Gotcha'. But what was it?

'Just a minute, Gwydion,' I muttered. 'I think he's managed to trick us, somehow.' I thought very hard about what Gwydion had said. I thought of the exact words. It all seemed perfectly fine. O'Liam's Mammy, Siobhan Flowerface, no attacking us as we left – hang on. I'd just seen the loopholes that had been obvious to the leprechaun's sneaky little mind.

'Before we agree to dine, Lord Conor,' I chipped in, hastily, 'Gwydion Dragonking meant to say "leave the Land Beneath *and Erin*" without being molested. Right, Gwydion?'

Gwydion went pale, suddenly. 'Yes, of course,' he stammered. 'That's what I meant.'

'But that isn't what you *said*,' Conor said smoothly. 'And we agreed what you *said*, did we not, so? You cannot change the terms now.'

So, we had no safe conduct once we were out of the Land Beneath. And if I knew Conor, every hazard – and there were many, many hazards of many, many kinds in Erin – was even at that moment being put on full alert to get us before we reached the coast. I also had a sneaky feeling it was going to get worse. 'And, Conor,' I went on, my fingers, toes, eyes and everything else crossed, 'what was the spell you actually put on Ynys Haf? If you don't mind telling us now you've agreed to our terms?'

'Oh, I don't mind at all, Lady Tan'ith,' he chortled. 'I put no spell at all on Ynys Haf. Whoever it was that enchanted your land, it was not me. No, not at all.'

'Oh, shoot!' I said. And believe it or not, I still hadn't even spotted the really glaring mistake. That was to come later…

'If it wasn't you,' Gwydion said miserably, 'then who was it?'

Conor shrugged. 'Who can say, Gwydion Dragonking? One such as you must have many enemies. But I give you my word as a leprechaun, it was not I.'

Not, of course, that his word as a leprechaun was worth a lot.

'Now,' he stood up, briskly. 'Business completed. 'You will fetch Maebh. Will you dine with me first, or will you go straight away?'

I had a funny feeling that if we ate with him, we might never leave the Land Beneath. 'No, thank you, Lord Conor,' I said firmly, 'we will visit O'Liam's Mammy, and then go and fetch Maebh. When we return with her, we shall take Siobhan Flowerface and go.'

O'Liam's face was glowing with delight: after all, he had exactly what he wanted, didn't he?

We followed O'Liam down a long corridor, with many twists and turns, until we came to a small doorway. Believe it or not, deep underground, there were roses twined round the door! O'Liam knocked once, and then opened the door.

In a rocking chair in the middle of the floor sat an ancient, tiny lady leprechaun. She looked about two thousand years old. Even her wrinkles had wrinkles. She rocked and knitted, and sang as she worked. All around her were Things: jewellery, ornaments, crockery, cutlery, swords, paintings, statues, books, pots and pans, furniture, everything you could think of. There was even (and I could hardly believe it) a garden gnome, with a fishing rod and a bunch of plastic flowers, though goodness knows where she'd got those from, because they certainly hadn't invented plastic yet.

'Mammy!' cried O'Liam, and the old lady put down her knitting to give him a hug.

'Is it yourself, O'Liam, my boy?'

'Oh, it is so, Mammy, it is so. And haven't I brought you some fine visitors, Mammy,' O'Liam said proudly. 'And I want you to be the first to know that Siobhan Flowerface and me are to be wed just as soon as I can find a broomstick for us to jump, so.'

The old lady twinkled. 'Have you spoken to Siobhan yet, O'Liam? Ah, I thought not, I thought not.' She stood up. She just about came up to Gwydion's thighs. He bowed politely, and she curtseyed back.

'Oh, I know who this is,' she said. 'Sure, and doesn't he have the look of his Mammy and his Daddy about him altogether from top to toe and all the many bits in between. His Daddy's height and his Mammy's lovely eyes as green as Erin's grass.' Gwydion went pink, I was glad to see. 'And I know who this is, too,' the tiny creature said, reaching up and holding my hand. 'You'll be Gwenhwyfar's daughter, will you not? Sure and you're the spit out of her mouth. Give me a hug, darlin'!'

I bent and hugged her. It was like hugging a dandelion clock, Her white hair tickled my nose and made me sneeze. When I opened my eyes again, Gwydion's hand was covering his mouth, hiding a huge grin.

O'Liam put his hands on his hips and surveyed his mother. 'Mammy! Did I not say that this is Gwydion Dragonking and the Lady of Ynys Haf? Sure, and aren't I First Leprechaun to the Dragonking? So would you please give back to the Lady the things you stole, Mammy, or I will not be able to look them in the eyes at all, ever?'

Stole? The old lady looked sulky. Then, out of her pocket she took my emerald pendant, the Arianrhod ring (how had she got that off without me feeling it go?) and from her knitting bag she produced my Ynys Haf coronet, my hanky that had been in my pocket, and an apple I'd saved from breakfast!

I shut my mouth, which had dropped open. Good grief, she'd be a whiz as a shoplifter in our Time!

'Thank you, Mammy. It's good to be polite, and it isn't polite at all to steal from friends.'

'I think it would be a good idea to get out of here as quickly as we can, O'Liam,' I suggested. 'And we still need to get Siobhan and her stuff ready to go.'

The old lady chuckled. 'Ah, yes, Siobhan, Siobhan, darlin' girl that she is to be sure.' And then she chuckled again.

'Mammy, will you give over laughing? It will cheer you immensely, so it will, to know that once a year I shall be back for a whole month. So even though I am being leprechaun to the Dragonking, I shall also be Ironfinder for Conor, and so I shall see you once a year, regular as cuckoos.'

The ancient leprechaun nodded, showing her gums in a toothless smile, and went back to her knitting. I waved goodbye. I wasn't getting close enough for her to half-inch my stuff again, but O'Liam gave her a hug and got a knitting needle up his nose for his trouble. Then we went to find Siobhan Flowerface.

22

We found Siobhan Flowerface in the kitchens, beating eggs so fast that her hand and wrist were a blur. The kitchens were busy as an ant-heap, presided over by an enormously fat lady leprechaun in a vast pinny, who was issuing orders and waving a wooden spoon like a conductor conducting an orchestra. Siobhan glanced up as we went in, and then went back to her eggs.

She was a tiny, black-haired little creature with dark golden skin and huge eyes as amber as an owl's She had a dear little nose (envy, envy!) and a rosebud mouth. Her hair was done in a thick plait over her right shoulder, and she should have, to my mind, at least, flung her whisk in the air and herself at O'Liam in delight. Wasn't he there to sweep her off her feet and marry her?

'Siobhan Flowerface?' O'Liam said nervously, taking off his fine green hat and mangling the feather between his hands. 'It is myself.'

'I can see that. What might you be wanting, O'Liam of the –' she glanced at his feet. '– fine green boots with the flashy-bits.'

'Ah, Siobhan, you know fine well I'm wanting to marry you.'

'Then want,' Siobhan said, whirling away with her bowl of eggs, 'must be your master.'

Gwydion and I exchanged looks. Hang about, I thought, this isn't going exactly to plan. I nudged the leprechaun. 'O'Liam, haven't you asked her before?'

'Why would I be doing that, Lady?'

I stared at him. 'Didn't you think it might be a good idea?'

'What for? She wouldn't look at me at all, no not at all.'

'You mean she doesn't love you the way you love her?'

'Now why would she love me? Sure and she doesn't know me hardly at all.'

'Let me get this straight, O'Liam. You are expecting Siobhan to leave here and come to Ynys Haf with you, and get married – and you haven't even got to know her?'

'Well, we've talked a time or two, and danced a time or two, and three Christmasses ago didn't I give her a kiss. But no, I can't honestly say I have got to know her well enough to ask her to marry me. Isn't that why we're here now at this particular minute, style of thing?'

I looked helplessly at Gwydion, who was grinning again. Trouble was, I knew just how Siobhan felt, being taken for granted. Wsn't Gwydion expecting me to be his Dragonqueen when the time was right? And had anyone ever asked me what I wanted to do?

'I thought you might have a word with her, Lady,' O'Liam muttered, scrubbing at a patch of flour on the floor with the toe of his boot. 'Doesn't she make me a wee bit nervous?'

'Who, me?' I looked at O'Liam's hopeful face. 'Oh, all right. Excuse me, Miss -um, Flowerface?'

Siobhan turned round, a scowl fixed to her pretty face. 'And who might you be, Lady? I can see you are important, so I can, by your fine clothes, but no one has introduced us at all, so I can't be knowing you.'

'Sorry. I'm Tan'ith, Lady of Ynys Haf, and this is Gwydion Dragonking, Lord of Ynys Haf.'

'Ooh!' she said, dropping a neat curtsy and batting her eyelashes at Gwydion. 'He's a fine big man, so he is. Would he be yours entirely?'

'More or less,' I admitted.

'Now that's a wee bit of a pity,' she said, showing her dimples.

I thought it best to let that one pass. 'O'Liam here,' I began, 'has asked me to tell you that he loves you and would like to marry you.'

She tossed her plait. 'Oh, has he indeed? He's not said a word the like to me.'

'I rather think you scare him, Siobhan.'

'Good. Well, you can tell the wee one in the fine green boots to stop killing the feather in his hat and ask me himself.'

'OK. Right.'

I went over to where O'Liam was trying to hide behind a cooking pot. 'She wants you to ask her yourself, O'Liam.'

He looked hopeful. 'Will she say yes if I do?'

'How do I know? But you'll never find out unless you ask her.' *And get on with it,* I thought, *I want to get out of here, quick.*

O'Liam sidled over to Siobhan. She bustled past him, waving a large cabbage under his nose. He cleared his throat noisily.

'Siobhan Flowerface,' he began nervously, 'would

you be doing me the honour of becoming my wife entirely and forevermore?'

'Why?' she asked.

O'Liam looked bewildered. 'Why? Wouldn't any style of man worth his salt like to have you as his wife, Siobhan?'

'And what style of any man are you, O'Liam of the Green Boots?'

O'Liam considered. 'I'm First Leprechaun to the Dragonking of Ynys Haf,' he boasted, 'and I'm O'Liam-once-a-year-for-a-month-Ironfinder-to-Conor-of-the-Land-Beneath.'

'So?'

'All these things, and I love you also, Siobhan Flowerface.'

The girl stood still. Then she smiled. 'Then I will marry you, O'Liam of the Green Boots.'

Gwydion and I smiled at each other. I was thinking, *Aaaaaah! There's sweet!* But then O'Liam fainted, and the next ten minutes were spent bringing him round. Once he'd recovered, and was sitting groggily on a stool grinning like a lovesick idiot, with Siobhan sitting next to him holding his hand, and the cook was weeping happy romantic tears in the corner, and all the kitchen maids were giggling excitedly over a glass of something very alcoholic to celebrate, I started to worry about getting out of there ever again.

'Look,' I said, 'I don't particularly want to hurry you, Siobhan, but we need to get away from here. I don't know how much stuff you have to pack, but I'd be really grateful if you could possibly go and pack it.'

Siobhan went like a bat out of hell, and half an hour later she was back with a small bag in her hand.

'Oh, great. Is that it?'

'It is not. Sure and aren't there a few more things back in my chamber that need to be fetched? O'Liam, will you go and get them for me?'

'Oh, I will so, my love!' O'Liam trotted happily off. He came back ten minutes later laden down with about ten different carpet-bags and boxes, puffing and red in the face.

'Good grief,' Gwydion groaned. 'How are we expected to get these back to Ynys Haf?'

'No problem. Once we've got them out of here I can magic them over.'

'They won't get lost in mid air, will they?' Siobhan asked anxiously. 'For isn't my granny's wedding dress all folded up in tissue paper in one of them bags.'

'They'll be safe enough,' I assured her. 'But I think we could do with getting them up above ground. And then, once I've organised the baggage, we'll go and get Maebh and bring her back to Conor.'

Of course, we had to leave O'Liam and Siobhan behind until we fetched her. Conor of the Land Beneath didn't trust us that much. So I said the spell that sent Siobhan's baggage on ahead (and wouldn't British Airways like to be able to do that with their passengers' luggage!) and then Gwydion and I set off to retrieve Maebh from the cave where we'd left her.

Would it surprise you to discover that she wasn't there? No, I didn't think it would. It certainly surprised me, but not as much as the note that was tucked under the rock instead of Maebh's string bag.

Deer Witch person

I av bin wotchin u. U av got my wun troo luv O'Liam. If u wont yor edgog bak I wil swop it 4 O'Liam. If u do not I wil bak it in clay wiv sum hurbs an ete it.

An I wil tel Deirdre u ar ere an she wil get u an kil u.

Cornelia the Bog Fairy

'Gwydion,' I said, 'things just got worse.' I handed him the note. 'I don't know about you, but I'm fed up with complications. It started out so simple, and now everything that can possibly go wrong, has.'

'No it hasn't,' he reminded me, 'we're still breathing?'

'There is that,' I admitted. 'But what do we do now?'

'We go and find Cornelia the Bog Fairy and try to do a deal with her.'

'Cornelia. I ask you. What a name for a Bog Fairy! Do you have any idea where she lives?'

He looked at me patiently. 'I would rather imagine that she lives in a bog, Tanz,' he said.

'Ireland, Gwydion, is full of bogs. Let's just hope that the bogs aren't full of Bog Fairies.'

'I don't think so. As far as I can remember, there's only ever one Bog Fairy at a time.'

I couldn't argue with that. So the two of us shifted into blackbirds and took to the skies over Erin looking for a bog. I was right. There are an awful lot of bogs in Ireland. However, I knew that Cornelia's bog wouldn't be too far away from Big Deirdre's cottage, because they were 'visiting neighbours'. Even so, it was getting quite dark when we finally spotted the small, tumbledown cottage made of slabs of peat, perched in the middle of a large bog. Tufts of coarse grass grew here and there and from above we could see that there were paths, but that it would be horribly easy to step off one, and drown in the bog. We landed on the Bog Fairy's roof and listened. She was singing a burbly, Bog Fairy type song. I fluttered down and peered in the window. Hedgehog Maebh was in a cage beside the hearth. There was a large, fragrant peat fire. Beside it was a bucket of clay. Possibly being baked in clay might be worse than spending the rest of eternity with Conor of the Land Beneath, but I wouldn't be prepared to bet on it. Once again, I began to feel sorry for Maebh.

I flew back up to Gwydion. 'She's in there, in a cage. How we're going to get her out I can't imagine. Any ideas?'

He put his small blackbird head on one side. 'Are you any good at imitations?'

'No.'

'Pity. You could have imitated O'Liam's voice and got the Bog Fairy to follow you away from the cottage while I nipped in and rescued Maebh.'

'Do you think she knows it's Maebh?'

He shook his head and fluffed up his breast feathers. 'She obviously knows it's something special, not just a hedgehog. But she can't possibly know what.'

I had an idea. 'I wonder if she's of a nervous disposition, Gwyd?'

'What do you mean?'

'Well, she doesn't know that the hedgehog is really a person, right? So if we turn Maebh back into Maebh, she's going to be shocked, right? And once Maebh is changed back, all we have to do is rush in and grab her.'

'Before she has time to shift into a magpie and fly away, you mean.'

'Yes. And then we leg it, and the Bog Fairy doesn't have the hedgehog any more.'

He looked as dubious as a blackbird possibly could. 'It *sounds* like a good idea, but –'

'Got any better ones? No? Right, then.'

We flew down and silently shifted to ourselves. I sidled round until I could see the hedgehog through the cottage window, and zapped the wooden cage so that the hedgehog was free. Then, I changed the hedgehog into Maebh and gave Gwydion the signal. He burst through the door, and made a grab at Maebh. Unfortunately, the Bog Fairy chose that time to turn round, spot Maebh, scream at the top of her voice, bump into Gwydion and knock him flat (she was almost as big as he was, after all). Gwydion toppled like a falling tree, bumped into me, and in the meantime Maebh changed into a magpie, shot through the window and was gone.

Gwydion and I picked ourselves up, and so did the Bog Fairy. She reached out a pair of hairy arms to grab us but in that instant we shifted back to blackbirds and flew out of the window after Maebh. Too long after Maebh. There was no sign of her.

23

And it was almost dark. The bats were zooming around, and darkness is no place for blackbirds.

'Now what?' I said miserably, shifting back to me.

Gwydion shot out of the blackbird-shape beside me. 'Ow!' he said, stretching his bad leg. 'That hurts. I think I bashed it when the Bog Fairy knocked me over.'

'I suppose we'd better rest, then, until morning. Then we can go and find Maebh.' So we shifted back into owls and flew out of the bog, up into the mountains and to the cave where we'd left Maebh some hours before. Gwydion built a fire, and I magicked up some sausages, onions, bread rolls and a frying pan, and we had hot dogs and canned rice pudding with strawberry jam for afters. I think it's called 'comfort food', and we certainly needed some comfort. It hadn't been a good day.

Afterwards, I curled up on a sleeping bag, and Gwydion sat upright beside me, feeding twigs into the crackling fire, the glow flickering on his face. From where I was, he was upside-down, of course.

'Gwydion?'

'Mm?'

'If Conor wasn't the one who put the enchantment on Ynys Haf, who do you think it was?'

'I've been thinking about that. At first, I thought that there were only two people it could possibly be. One is Merlin, and he wouldn't do it. And the other is Master Henbane. But there is another possibility, of course.'

‘There is?’

‘Conor was lying.’

I thought about that. ‘No. He was quite straightforward about that, at least. “Whoever it was that enchanted your land”, he said, “it was not me”. You can’t get round that, even if he is a sneaky little so-and-so. It wasn’t him. So I suppose it has to be Henbane. The trouble is, I didn’t think he was ever really strong enough to do something like that. I mean, it takes a major wizard or witch to put an entire kingdom under a weather spell. And Astarte’s gone, Maebh isn’t strong enough, and Rhiryd Goch’s sons wouldn’t have a clue how to go about it. The Great Druid might have managed it, in about twenty years and after a lot of vitamins, but he was still out for the count when I looked. That only leaves *Merch Corryn Du* – Spiderwitch herself. And the dragon took her, right?’

‘Mm. Bugsy.’

‘That was Bugsy? Wrapped around the castle?’

‘Well, of course it was! How many dragons of that size do you think there are left in Ynys Haf?’

‘Why is he called Bugsy?’

‘Oh, it’s a long story. Goes back to when Bugsy was a baby and I was about ten. I’ll tell you some day. It’s quite a funny story.’

‘Anyway, it couldn’t possibly be the Spiderwitch, could it?’

He went very quiet.

‘Gwydion? It couldn’t poss-’

‘I heard you. And I don’t know. Because you see, although Bugsy carried her off, I never found out exactly what he did with her. I sort of assumed he'd – um – disposed of her. But if he didn't, then –'

'So she could still be alive?' I sat up and stared at him.

'Could be. And besides, Bugsy has taken to flying over the camp, night after night, as if he is trying to talk to me.'

'Dragons talk?'

'No, of course not. But I think perhaps he might be trying to tell me something. He doesn't usually visit this often – he's usually too busy. I've been in such a state since I got wounded –'

'You're telling me,' I said feelingly.

'I haven't really paid much attention to anything else. And anyway, Tanz, the other thing is we don't know exactly who turned the Oldway Creatures loose, do we?'

'Well, I assumed it was Conor. But then, he didn't mention it, did he, and he is the sort of person who likes to rub it in when he can, right?'

'Right. So maybe – just maybe, it might be the Spiderwitch.'

'So what do we do next? Do we leave O'Liam and Siobhan behind, go back to Ynys Haf and sort things out there, or do we carry on looking for Maebh so we can get O'Liam out, or what?'

Gwydion shrugged. 'Let's decide in the morning.' And then he wriggled inside his sleeping bag, turned on his side, and within seconds, was snoring.

I lay there for a bit, but I couldn't sleep. Ideas were whizzing round in my head. Surely he was wrong, surely it couldn't be *Merch Corryn Du* back to haunt us, could it? I shivered. Then I started thinking about

Maebh, and wondering where she'd got to. Would she head back to the dilapidated Irish castle where we'd found her and Henbane? She might, but then when she found Henbane wasn't there, what would she do then? All that thinking was giving me a headache. And if we found her, I still wasn't entirely sure I could bring myself to hand her over to Conor. But unfortunately, I couldn't see any way around it.

The next thing that popped into my brain was T.A. That little smile Conor had on his face when he said that about T.A. staying with him of her own free will. What was all THAT about? T.A. was in Ynys Haf, and he didn't have a hope of getting hold of her. So what was he up to?

Something moved below us on the mountainside, dislodging pebbles and sending them clattering down into the valley. I squirmed out of my bag and peered over the edge, but couldn't see anything. Probably just a fox or something out hunting. But the small sound had woken Gwydion.

'Tanz?' he whispered.

'Mm?'

'What was that noise?'

'Don't know. I can't see anything. It's stopped now, anyway.'

'Oh.' There were settling down noises from his direction.

'Gwydion?'

'What?'

'I'm –' What was I? Scared? No. Lonely? A bit. Worried? A lot. 'Doesn't matter.'

There was a short silence from the patch of firelight

where the Dragonking of Ynys Haf was snuggled in a bright orange sleeping-bag. Then there was a wriggling noise, and like an over-sized grub, he wriggled towards me. He kissed the end of my nose, put his arm across me and snuggled down beside me.

'Better?'

'Much.'

Strangely, I was able to sleep quite quickly after that.

Next morning, the sun woke us, shining directly into the mouth of the cave. I opened my eyes and squinted into the red glare. Gwydion was up and about already, and he had built up the fire. A pair of fine river trout were sizzling over the flames, and they made a wonderful breakfast. Once we had eaten and disposed of the debris and the sleeping bags, we had to decide what to do.

'I think we have to try to find Maebh,' he decided. 'I don't want to go back to Ynys Haf without O'Liam, and if we did leave him behind we'd only have to come back to get him. I don't think Maebh can have left Erin, and if we can find her, we can decide what to do next.'

'We take her to Conor, and leave her to a horrible life, for ever and ever,' I said miserably.

Gwydion glanced at me, under his eyebrows. 'Isn't that what we said we'd do?'

I nodded. 'The trouble is, Gwydion, that I can't help feeling sorry for her. She's been pushed around and sort of used all her life, first by Spiderwitch, then by Astarte – she wasn't very kind to her when she was her magpie, was she? And then Master Henbane got his hooks into her and lied to her. Promised she could be Queen when he had no intention of letting her be anything of the sort. He just used her because she was a pretty face, that's all. He knew that people would say yes to her when they would have made him pack his bags and hop it. And now we're supposed to turn her over to Conor to get his revenge on her because she turned him down. It doesn't seem right, somehow.'

'I agree she's had a pretty horrible life, Tanz. But she isn't very bright, or she wouldn't have let all those people use her like that.'

'She can't help being a dumb bunny, Gwyd.'

'So, what are you going to do about it? I can't see any way around it, unless you're prepared to abandon O'Liam and Siobhan. Can you?'

Miserably, I shook my head. But I was going to go on thinking about it. It just didn't seem right that the future Dragonqueen of Ynys Haf was going to do something as nasty as that.

Anyway, first we had to find her. We decided that the most likely place she'd head for would be the old castle. We shifted into rooks and took to the skies, tumbling in the updraughts, rolling in the wind the way rooks do. After a while, the wind dropped, and I noticed that, on the far horizon, great banks of clouds were piling, dark and heavy. It looked as if the Emerald Isle was about to get a little rain.

'Look at that, Gwyd,' I squawked. 'We'd better hurry up and find Maebh before that lot hits us.'

The air became hot and oppressive, even high in the air, and there was that peculiar light that heralded a thunderstorm. We quickened our flight and headed for the castle. The clouds built up and up, massive black thunderheads, and the sky lost any trace of blue and turned to a septic sort of yellow. I couldn't help noticing that small animals were heading for burrows, and birds were taking shelter in thick trees. As storms go, this one would be a big one. The animals could tell. Even I, a fake creature, could feel the electricity tingling through my feathers.

We were in sight of the castle when the storm hit. First there was an almighty, searing flash of lightning, and then the sky reverberated with thunder, deafening, violent, shuddering the air around us. It rolled down one side of the valley and up the other, and as the sound died away there was another flash and another rumble, almost on top of us.

Gwydion swooped down into an arrowslit in a turret, closely followed by me, and just as the heavens opened and the rain fell out of the sky as if someone had turned on a tap, we got under cover. We perched close to each other for comfort, and watched, as the storm raged overhead. It was like having a personal thunderstorm, because it didn't seem to be moving away. It sort of stuck over the castle and ranted and roared. In a pause between the rumbles of thunder there was a huge strike of sheet lightning, that turned the sky a vibrant electric blue. It hit a tree which almost exploded with energy, catching fire and toppling.

As the crash of its falling died away, I heard the other noise.

'Listen, Gwydion!' I said urgently. 'Can you hear that?'

He could. Inside the castle a voice was screaming hysterically, on and on and on, as if seven devils and fifty-four banshees were having a screeching match.

'Come on,' he said, and dropped down through the ruined walls in the direction of the voice.

We flitted through empty rooms full of rotting furniture and mouldy wall-hangings, perched on fallen interior walls and listened, and then took off again in the direction of the screams. They got louder and louder, until, in a chamber half-way up a tall tower, we found the owner of the voice.

Maebh. She was crouched in a corner underneath a broken, three-legged table, her cloak thrown over her head, her hands over her ears, screaming so loud that she didn't hear us coming. She was shaking her head wildly, side to side, as if to shake out the noise that was battering at her. Because her eyes were shut she didn't see us, either, and so we were able to land and shift before she had any idea we were there.

'She's terrified, Gwydion!' I whispered. 'She's afraid of the storm.' I stepped forward and gathered the girl into my arms. Sobbing hysterically, she clung to me, not caring who or what I was, just so afraid that any sort of comfort was better than none. Gwydion put his arms round both of us and we stayed that way, holding the trembling girl, while the storm racketed and raged around us.

Until lightning struck the tower we were in, and the world began to wobble.

24

'The tower's going to collapse!' Gwydion yelled. 'Come on, quick!'

He picked Maebh up and slung her over his shoulder. She was still screaming, and I found myself patting and shushing her as we careered down the spiral staircase. Bits of plaster were falling from the roof, and stones were popping out of the walls. The air was filled with a great groaning, rending noise as ancient mortar crumbled away. The tower seemed to be shifting under our feet as we ran, making me reel with giddiness. I can tell you, it isn't fun belting down a spiral staircase that's *moving*.

'Thank goodness she wasn't at the top of the tower,' Gwydion panted, taking the spiral steps two at a time.

'Pity she wasn't at the bottom,' I yelled.

We reached the tower doorway just in time, hurtled into the courtyard and through the pelting rain across to the other side, where we stood in the shelter of the gatehouse. There we watched open-mouthed as the great tower twisted, swayed and slowly collapsed in on itself with a mighty roar of falling masonry.

'Crumbs!' I said. 'That was a close one!'

Maebh had stopped screaming (it's hard to scream when your middle section is being bounced on top of a hard shoulder). Gwydion put her down, and leaned her against the wall, which she slithered down. Her eyes were still tightly shut, and she was whimpering.

I bent over her and patted her where she sat in the mud. 'It's all right now, Maebh. You're safe.'

'I'm not safe. I'll never be safe. Isn't the whole entire world out to get me?'

It probably felt that way. 'I think that's called paranoia, Maebh,' I said gently. 'It's just a thunderstorm.'

'And who sent it, that's what I'd like to know? Was it Conor of the Land Beneath? Master Henbane? The Lady of Ynys Haf?'

'I don't actually think anyone sent it, Maebh. Thunderstorms happen, right? This one happened to us the same way as it happened to you. And I know I didn't send it.'

She suddenly stopped whimpering and went very still. 'I? Who is I?' She opened one eye and then shut it again, quickly. 'Oh, no, the very thing I feared! The witch has got me! I knew I should not have ignored the tingling of my nose. But I was so afraid of the thunderclaps I did not think further, I did not. Oh, dear. It's the end for me, to be sure. My last moment is upon me.'

There, now I was feeling like a baddie again. 'It's all right, Maebh,' I insisted. 'Would we have rescued you from the tower if we didn't want you alive?'

'We? That means there is more than one I, does it not. Who is the other I?' She opened both her eyes and looked round, this time catching sight of Gwydion. 'Oh, no, if it isn't the Dragonking himself. This is certainly my final hour, for did Master Henbane not make me Queen of his country when the Dragonking was still on this earth?'

Gwydion was patting her now, looking just as worried as I felt. 'Look, calm down, Maebh. You're all right for the moment. I'm not out to get revenge on you for something Henbane did. Don't worry.'

'Don't worry!' she shrieked, slapping his hand away. 'Don't worry, the man says! And if he isn't going to be killing me now he'll kill me later. Or he'll do something to me that's worse, that's for sure.'

Trouble was, she was right. I had a feeling that handing her over to Conor was going to be worse. Everything we said only tied us further into knots of guilt. I was going to have to be tough. I was going to have to tell it like it was. If getting O'Liam and Siobhan out of the Land Beneath meant that Maebh had to be sacrificed, then so be it. 'Look, Maebh,' I said sternly, prepared to say that if she had to be turned over to Conor then it was her tough luck for getting mixed up with baddies. Unfortunately, what actually came out of my mouth was 'Look, Maebh. No one is going to hand you over to Conor against your will. We'll find some way around it, I promise.'

Gwydion looked at me with his mouth open.

'What?' I said. 'What? What did I say?'

'Oh, Tanz!' he groaned. 'Now you've done it!'

I probably had, too. What was the matter with me, making a promise like that?

'Sorry, Gwyd,' I said, miserably. 'I just couldn't bear to –'

He patted my shoulder. 'I know. Didn't anyone ever tell you that you have to be ruthless to rule?'

'I'm not ruling, yet,' I said, grinning, 'you are.'

'Not very well, apparently,' he said ruefully.

'We've both got L-plates up, Gwyd. But we'll

learn. In the meantime, that's another fine mess I've got us into, right?'

'Right.'

And strangely enough, with Maebh watching with an expression of complete bafflement on her face, Gwydion and I fell about laughing, howling until the tears ran down our faces and our sides ached. Eventually the howls subsided into muffled giggles, the giggles into snorts, and the snorts into grins that kept threatening to start up again, and all against a background of torrential rain and diminishing rumbles of thunder as the storm passed over.

Once the last giggle had gone, I dried my eyes on my sleeve. We sploshed out of the turret through great puddles that were reflecting the beginnings of a clear blue sky, and breathed in the newly fresh air. Maebh trailed after us miserably.

'Did you mean what you said, Dragonqueen?' she asked timidly. 'Will you not harm me?'

'I'm not Dragonqueen yet,' I reminded her. 'And no, we won't harm you.'

'And you will not give me to Conor of the Land Beneath?'

I sighed. 'No, we won't. I promised, and so I shan't. But in return you've got to promise us that you won't run away, and you won't get tangled up with Henbane again, or do anything to work against us.'

'But Master Henbane is powerfully persuasive when he puts his mind to it, he is so.'

'Nevertheless, Maebh,' Gwydion said sternly, 'you have to promise.'

'Then I promise,' she said, smiling prettily and

fluttering her eyelashes at him. It crossed my mind that I could like her a lot more, forgive her a lot more, if only she weren't so flipping pretty!

'The question is,' I reminded Gwydion, 'what do we do with her? And how can we get O'Liam and Siobhan out without sending Maebh in?'

He shrugged. 'I think we'd better have a good think about that. Perhaps you should consult your Spellorium. Maybe you could see if you could scry your Aunt Ant, or your mother, to see if they have any ideas.'

Well, it was a place to start, at least. The birds were beginning to come out of hiding, now that the storm had passed, and when a blackbird flew past with a fat worm in her beak, it gave me an idea.

'I think I know where we can stash Maebh until we decide what to do with her,' I said. 'Somewhere she'll be perfectly safe. If he's not otherwise engaged, of course.'

I didn't think it would be a good idea to shift Maebh quite so soon after her ordeal by terror and thunderstorm, and to be honest I felt a bit wobbly myself, so we walked to where I wanted to go. He was still there, sitting on his crag, but his arms were folded and his hands were empty. He looked sad. He was also dripping wet, having apparently sat there throughout the thunderstorm.

'Good afternoon, Brother Kevin,' I greeted him. 'How are you?'

'Oh, is it yourself, Lady?' he said, brightening at the prospect of some company. 'Oh, I am so. But my babies flew away and I feel empty as an eggshell, I do.' He spread his hands and looked helpless. 'Sure, I don't know what to do with myself.' He wiped a drip off his nose, and then looked at his hands as if he didn't quite know what use they were any more.

Gwydion was looking bewildered, so I explained about the friar and the blackbird's eggs.

'And now they've left I can't find it in myself to move at all. I may stay here on my rock until I die,' Kevin sighed. 'Haven't I sat here all the day with the lightning and the thunder bouncing about the sky?'

'What if I could find you someone else to look after, Brother Kevin?' I suggested.

'Ah, it is only once in a lifetime a blackbird trusting enough will lay eggs in a man's hand,' he sighed. 'Once in a long, long lifetime does a privilege like that happen.'

'But there's someone else who needs your help. If you will give it,' I said.

'And who might that be?'

I grabbed hold of Maebh's sleeve and yanked her forward. 'This lady is in distress, Brother Kevin, and I would be so grateful if you could look after her for a while, until we come back and get her.'

Brother Kevin looked at Maebh, and Maebh looked at Brother Kevin. She was tear-stained, wet, bedraggled, and very, very pretty. She flashed her dimples and blushed. A rain-drop trickled down her cheek from one of her curls. Brother Kevin melted.

'You will not be nesting in the palm of my hand, lady,' he said, 'but I shall take care of you just like a little bird in my little house, so I will.' He put his arm around Maebh's shoulders and led her away towards a little house nestled at the foot of the crag. 'I shall feed you on butter and cream, and soon you will be well and strong again. Leave the maid with me, Lady. I shall take care of her, I promise I shall, so.' Maebh was looking up at him and telling him her troubles.

'She'll be perfectly safe with him,' I said, satisfied. 'And she won't dare to do anything to upset someone who's bound to be a saint one day. So she'll behave herself and stay put until we decide what to do with her. Besides, I think even Maebh knows when she's well off. AND she's promised.'

Gwydion shook his head helplessly. 'And in the meantime, we have to decide what to do about Conor.'

'We do so!' I said, imitating O'Liam. 'We do so.'

He aimed a mock punch at my nose and grinned at me. 'Now, I think it would be a good idea to find a nice, still pool and see what we can see.'

It took a while's flying to find one, but eventually we found a good one, a still surface of brown water trapped in a hollow. It would drain as the ground dried out, but after the storm, it was held there perfectly, reflecting the blue sky. I got down on my knees and leaned over it, took a deep, deep breath and blew it softly on the water.

As I blew, a mist formed over the pool, faint at first, and then thicker and thicker, boiling up from the clear, still water and then clearing gradually away.

I waved the last few wisps away and peered in. Mam and Aunt Ant were together, sitting in our front room eating sponge cake and drinking tea. Cariad was in her play-pen screaming her head off from the look of the open mouth and red face, but Mam wasn't taking any notice of her grand-daughter. She knew she was safer away from hot teapots. Suddenly, Cariad's silent screams (there's no audio on scrying!) stopped, and she pointed up, directly at me. Mam looked up first, and then Aunt Ant, and I knew that they had been talking about me, otherwise they would not have known I was there. I waved and smiled, and Gwydion waved over my shoulder.

Mam patted her chest, showing relief, and then she dived out of sight for a second and came up with my crystal ball. She waved it at me. She was telling me that she had been watching what had been going on. She knew, then. Good.

I mouthed at her 'What can I do about Maebh?'

Mam mouthed something back, but I couldn't get it. I cupped my hand behind my ear and shrugged to show I hadn't understood. She mouthed it again, and still I didn't get it. Then Aunt Ant got up, and rushed away. She came back a couple of seconds later and waved something at me. I stared, not understanding, and then I saw what it was she was waving.

And I still didn't understand. And then a frog leapt into the pool and the picture was gone.

'Drat!' I said, with feeling. (Actually I said something else, but I won't repeat it). 'What on earth does she mean by that?'

25

'What was it?' Gwydion asked, as puzzled as I was.

'A corn dolly,' I said. 'One of those symbols woven out of corn that you get at craft fairs. Well, you don't. But we do, in our Time.'

'Well, it must mean something, Tanz. But what?'

'How should I know?'

'Your mother must have thought you would know, or she would have been a bit more specific, don't you think? So why don't you rustle up something to eat, and while we're eating, try to work out what she means by it.'

'So I get to rustle up and think, do I? And what do you do while I'm doing all the work?'

'Work? Magicking some food onto our plates?'

'Exactly.'

'All right, I'll do the magicking. But no moaning if you don't like what I get, all right?'

I wish I'd done it myself. I mean, jellied eels and ale? Yuk. I took one look at the horrid things and produced a double-decker burger and fries. And coke.

'Do you honestly like those things, Gwydion?' I asked, tucking in.

'No. I can't stand them, actually. I only did it to make you pull a face. Can I have some of your burger?'

'No. Oh, all right.' I magicked another one and we settled down. Him to munch, me to think. Corn dollies. Corn dollies. Corn dollies. What on earth was the use of corn dollies?

I picked a bit of tomato out of my double-decker and nibbled at it. Corn dollies. I munched on a bit of lettuce. Corn dollies. I wiggled a pickle out of the middle and chomped on it. Corn dollies. I dunked a fry in tomato ketchup and chewed it. Corn dollies. I slurped on my coke. Corn dollies.

When I'd finished, I screwed up the paper wrappings and threw them into the air. They vanished before they hit the ground. Corn dollies.

I magicked some large, juicy nectarines and ripe strawberries and shared them with Gwydion. Corn dollies.

I lay back against a tree and concentrated. Corn dollies. No. Not one single glimmer of an idea. Corn dollies. I thought about the little gleaming magic book that the Lady had given me. Nothing in there about corn dollies.

Then I went through the Emerald Spellorium from cover to cover in my mind. Nothing at all in there about corn dollies. No dollies at all. Not even any corn. Only straw.

STRAW! 'Gwydion,' I said slowly, sitting up, 'Gwydion, I think I've got it!'

'What?' he mumbled. He was falling asleep, the wretch, and leaving me to worry. I kicked his ankle, hard.

'Ow!' This time, he sat up. 'What?'

'It isn't corn dollies. It's golems.'

'Pardon?'

'Golems. Do you know what a golem is?'

Gwydion shook his head. Ha! Something he didn't know, at last! I knew all that reading for my English course-work on the Twentieth-Century Short Story would pay off!

'Pay attention,' I ordered. 'A golem is a Jewish legend. It's an artificial human being brought to life by supernatural means. Sometimes it's made of mud with human hair in it, or fingernail clippings. Sometimes it's made of straw…'

'But you aren't Jewish,' he said, mystified.

'I know that, dumbo. But we can make artificial people too. Oh, they don't last very long, but they can be made to look just as lifelike as you or me. Or Maebh. And if I can manage to make one of those, then it will give us time to get O'Liam and Siobhan away from Conor.'

'Isn't that cheating?'

'Yes. But I've asked myself, do I feel guilty about cheating Conor? And no, I don't. He's such a savage little beast. I won't give him Maebh. I don't care how upset he gets. And now I know that it isn't him wrecking the climate of Ynys Haf, I don't care. Are you with me, Gwydion?'

He grinned. 'Of course. I knew you could do it if you put your mind to it, Tanz!'

'We'll need some bits of Maebh. Hair, nails, stuff like that. And some straw and some mud. Come on.'

We shifted back into rooks and hurtled back to Kevin's little sod hut. There was a delicious smell of cooking coming from the open half-door, and inside Kevin was bustling about with pinny on, and a spoon in his hand. Maebh was sitting beside the fire, her curls brushed, stitching a rip in Kevin's old brown robe.

'Is it yourselves?' the friar said delightedly as we shifted. 'Will you stay and have a drop to eat? Ah you will, won't you? You will?'

'We've eaten, thanks,' I said. 'Maebh, we need to ask a favour.'

She put down her sewing and folded her hands in her lap. Her little feet were crossed at the ankles and she looked like an illustration for 'Little Miss Muffet' in a nursery rhyme book. She put her head prettily on one side and said, 'What might that be?'

'We want a piece of your hair, please, and some clipping from your fingernails.

She scowled. 'What would you be wanting those for? Are you going to put a spell on me? I know that spell. Didn't my granny teach it to me? It's the one where, if a witch has such stuff, you are in her power. I don't want to be in your power, I do not, not at all. Tell them to go away, Brother Kevin, tell them, please? They're frightening me again!' She squeezed out a couple of crystalline tears and Brother Kevin put down his spoon and rushed to protect her.

'No, it isn't that at all,' I protested. 'Honestly it isn't. I give you my word.'

'There, sweetling,' Brother Kevin said, patting her. 'Nothing to worry about. Will I fetch a little knife to cut a curl, then?'

'No, no, not my curls!' she shrieked.

I was beginning to stop feeling sorry for her. 'Oh, for goodness sake,' I muttered. 'Will you listen to her! What *is* she like?'

Gwydion dropped to one knee beside her chair. 'Look, Maebh. We truly don't want to hurt you.' He was using his terribly polite, terribly sympathetic voice which actually meant he was feeling exactly the opposite. 'We need these little bits of hair and stuff so that we don't have to send you back to Conor of the Land Beneath, all right? We're trying to help you, not harm you, I promise.'

'Conor of the Land Beneath?' Brother Kevin said, turning pale. 'Is that little nasty weasel involved in this whole thing? Oh, then, give his Lordship your hair, wee Maebh. All of it if necessary. Sure, and won't it grow again quick, and you be just as pretty? Even if you was bald entirely,' he finished loyally.

'All of it? No, no!' she shrieked and grabbed her hair as if we were going to shave it all off. I was very tempted, actually.

'No,' Gwydion said, gently (although by now a note of irritation was just beginning to creep in), 'just this little tiny curly bit by here. Underneath all the rest, so it will be hidden and won't spoil your looks at all.'

'Promise?' she said, dimpling at him.

'Promise,' he said sweetly, and quick as a flash he had his knife out and the curl cut off. 'And now one of your pretty, shell-like fingernails?'

Maebh spread out her fingers. 'Not that one,' she said. 'That's my nice long one. And not that one, for that one's next to it exactly, and almost as good. Not that one – how about a little wee bit off the smallest one of all?'

'That will do nicely,' Gwydion said through gritted teeth, and he whipped it off with his knife before she could complain.

'And now, a bit of your dress, and a bit of mud off your shoe,' I said, waiting for her to complain.

She opened her mouth, but it was too late. I had grabbed Gwydion's knife and hacked off the hem of her dress, and yanked her left leg up in the air to get at her shoe. I wrapped the mud and the other stuff in the piece of her dress, and that was it. All we needed now was the straw.

'Would you have some straw around anywhere?' I asked Brother Kevin. He thought about it. His face fell.

'I do not,' he said. 'But I know someone who will find me some.' He went to the door of the cottage, stuck his head out of the top half of the door, and whistled. A blackbird flew down, and he whistled again. She flew away, and a few minutes later came back with a beakful of straw.

That would do fine. I could magic the rest, once I had some real straw to work with. I could have magicked all the ingredients, but for this spell they had to be the real thing.

'Thanks,' I said, gratefully. 'With any luck, Maebh, this will get you off the hook entirely.'

Gwydion and I shifted and left. 'Not entirely,' Gwydion said as we flew towards the Land Beneath. 'Only a temporary fix. I just hope it holds long enough for us to get away.'

I couldn't answer without losing the square of cloth in my beak. But I thought. *It's got to, Gwydion. Or we're in deep, deep fertiliser!*

We halted in the woods a little way away from the entrance to the Land Beneath, and shifted back to our own shapes. I opened the square of Maebh's dress material and sorted out the mud, the straw, the hair and the nail clippings. I magicked a large double-handful of straw, and a bit more mud to mix with the rest, found a large leaf and put the mud on it. I added the hair and the fingernail and squidged it up. Then I made a rough human shape out of the straw, tying it like one of those woolly dolls you make from scraps of knitting wool: a long bunch of strands bent over, tied round the neck to form a head. Another bunch threaded through to form arms, and then tied round below it to make a waist. Then I squashed the mud into the body part, and a bit more into the head part, wrapped the square of material around it for a skirt and made sure some of the strands of hair were in the head part. Then I laid it on the ground.

This was the hard part. First I had to make it life-size. I concentrated hard, holding both my ears to help. (I don't know why holding my ears helps me concentrate, it just does. You should try it sometimes. It really works!) Suddenly the straw dolly on the ground twitched and began to grow. Great. That was step one taken care of. Now for the hard part.

> *Gyda gwallt ac ewin, brethyn a llaid*
> *Gwna debygrwydd da o Maebh!*

> With hair and fingernail, cloth and mud
> Make a good likeness of Maebh!

The spell continued

> May it breathe and move and speak
> And see and hear
> For at least a week!

Then I said a very strange, old-Welsh word that you really don't want to know about, one that is said only in very strange and dire circumstances. Anyway, it did the trick. The life-sized straw doll went fuzzy round the edges, blurred, twitched, and a strange fog rose from the ground to cover it. I sat back on my heels and watched. I clutched Gwydion's ankle for courage, because I was shaking. Making a false human being is desperate magic, and I only want to have to do it ever, once in my lifetime. And this was it.

When the fog cleared, there, lying on the ground, was a sort of photocopy of Maebh. The only trouble was, she was fast asleep, and whatever we did to wake her up, she stayed that way.

'Do you think,' I said, after a while, 'that Conor would believe she was very, very tired?'

'Maybe she is,' Gwydion said. 'Perhaps if we let her sleep, maybe she'll wake up of her own accord. Or when she's hungry. Otherwise, Tanz, I think we're stuck.'

So, we waited. And when we'd done that, we waited some more.

26

While she was sleeping I magicked some quite decent clothes onto her to replace the ragged scrap of a dress that had formed from the bit of the real Maebh's hem.

The straw-Maebh just lay there, a dark crescent of lashes on the creamy cheek, her lips parted over even white teeth, breathing gently in and out. And sleeping. And sleeping. I was beginning to wonder darkly about getting Gwydion to give her a kiss, see if that woke her up (you know, Sleeping Beauty sort of thing), but decided that would be altogether too much.

Would she ever wake up? Then she did. Talk about lifelike! She sat up, stretched, rolled over, and yawned. Prettily, of course, revealing a pink little tongue like a cat's.

She smiled, sweetly, and got up, and looked at us enquiringly. It really was uncanny how like Maebh she was: right down to the dimples. Now all we had to do was get her into the Land Beneath, fool Conor, and then get O'Liam and Siobhan out before Conor cottoned on to the fact that we had fooled him.

I didn't think it would be a good idea to try to shift her into anything to get to the Land Beneath. She wasn't real, after all, and I didn't want to risk upsetting the magic that was keeping her together, and so we set out to walk. She tripped along daintily, holding her skirt above her ankles, smiling happily. I didn't think there was much of a brain in there (but then, she hadn't had much to begin with, had she?), and I couldn't remember if straw-dolly people could talk. Certainly she wasn't contributing anything at all to the conversation – but Gwydion and I weren't very talkative either. I couldn't get my mind off the meeting to come, and hoping everything would go well.

We reached the Land Beneath and hammered on the door, since O'Liam wasn't there to open it for us. After a short wait the door swung back on its hinges and a short, fat leprechaun with a bad-tempered expression appeared. He glanced at the three of us (we had rapidly magicked our posh clothes on while we were waiting, so I was in full court-dress with my coronet). Then he tutted disapprovingly and set off at great speed down the winding corridors that led to the Land Beneath with us galloping behind.

Conor was waiting for us in his Throne Room. I was quite pleased by that, because I had been afraid that if he was having his dancing lesson or something, we'd be there too long, and that might have caused problems with straw dolly Maebh. The last thing we wanted to happen was for her to change back to a pile of dry grass, hair, and nail clippings before we'd got safely away with Conor's hostages. I certainly didn't want to be around when Conor discovered we had tricked him.

Conor was dressed in a rich suit of red, shimmering cloth, his huge, liquid eyes in the golden face surveying each step that we took as we walked towards him, Maebh between us, tripping along, still with the same bright smile on her face. My stomach was churning and I really was getting very keen to be away from there.

'Well, Dragonking. I see that you, unlike your

Lady, have kept your side of the bargain. You have brought me the Lady Maebh.'

Craftily, Gwydion didn't say anything. He just bowed and smiled. So he didn't have to lie, did he?

'Lady Maebh,' Conor took her fingertips and kissed them. 'I trust you are well?'

The fake Maebh looked brightly at Gwydion and me, and like noddy head dogs we nodded frantically, hoping she'd get the idea. She imitated us, nodding and smiling at Conor.

'And you, Lady of Ynys Haf. You have managed to overcome your squeamishness about giving me Maebh?'

I'm not daft. I did exactly as Gwydion had done. Bowed and smiled, as sincerely as I could manage.

Conor took the straw Maebh by the hand as if he were about to lead her in a gavotte or something, into the middle of the room, where a great chandelier threw a flickering candelight over the pair, shining in the blackness of her hair and shimmering on his dark crimson suit. His skin gleamed and his eyes danced. Dropping her fingers, he walked slowly all round her, as if he was inspecting a statue – or a cow. She turned with him, holding his eyes, still with the same bright, unknowing smile on her face, spinning, spinning.

'At last!' he breathed, 'I have you, Maebh. Oh, how I shall make you welcome. You shall never leave me again. Never. Do you understand?'

And the fake Maebh smiled and nodded, and her dimples danced.

Conor nodded, satisfied. 'You have kept your bargain, Lady of Ynys Haf. You may take the

Ironfinder and his woman,' he said, smiling. 'But do not forget: he must return once a year for one month to be my Ironfinder once more. And you will not, I am certain, forget the final clause of our agreement?'

'How could I forget it, Conor of the Land Beneath?' I asked. 'If the Lady Haf comes to you and stays of her own free will, then I promise that I will allow her to stay. I say again: if the lady Haf comes to you of her own accord, and if she wishes to stay, then of course she must. I have no argument with that at all.' *For a start, she wouldn't even think about you twice,* I thought. *And if she did, she certainly wouldn't want to pay you a visit! Not after last time.* So I was quite sure that making that particular promise was perfectly safe. Hadn't T.A. herself said she'd rather poke herself in the eye with a sharp stick? Well, then. She was about as likely to pay Conor a visit willingly as I was.

'And you will hold to that promise?' Conor said pointedly. 'For you are not remarkably good at keeping promises, I seem to recall.'

I blushed, I couldn't help it. 'I have brought you the lady you wanted,' I said, as firmly as I could manage (I'm such a BAD LIAR!). I deliberately didn't name her: I just called her 'the lady'. I hoped he wouldn't notice. 'I can say honestly that she is without any magic of her own, just as I promised. And I repeat. If Lady Haf comes to you of her own free will, travelling under her own steam, so to speak, and wishes to stay, then she may. There. I've said it twice. Does that satisfy you?'

Conor's smile was like a sunbeam coming out. 'Oh,

it does so. It does so, Lady! For a promise made twice, before witnesses, is a promise that can be broken only at your peril. Your very great peril.' He raised the fake Maebh's hand and kissed the fingers, one by one, all the time staring at me with his huge eyes.

'And now,' Gwydion said, smoothly, 'if you will allow us, we will take O'Liam of the Green Boots and his lady, and leave.'

'You may go. I have enjoyed your visit so very much,' Conor said. 'So very, very much. It will be a while before you discover quite how much, I am sure. But when you find out, it will give you a warm glow, it will so. And you will think of me often, when you have left here. That is my promise to you, Lady of Ynys Haf.'

What? I thought. Me think of him? Unlikely, unless it was the way I thought about tarantulas and rattlesnakes – glad I wasn't near him. But all the same, I had a sudden vague feeling of something happening that I wasn't exactly aware of. But what?

Then O'Liam and Siobhan arrived, hand in hand, and the fat, bad-tempered leprechaun came to take us back to the surface, and we were out of the Land Beneath, having accomplished everything and given nothing. We had O'Liam and Siobhan, and I had not sacrificed Maebh to Conor's malice. I had managed to cheat Conor of the Land Beneath of his awful revenge, which, since leprechauns are such sneaky little people, was quite something. On the whole, I felt pretty good about myself. It was just – I don't know. There was something about Conor's last words that niggled slightly. Nah. Maybe he was just being nice. I know

Conor wasn't nice naturally, but hey, hadn't we just brought him Maebh?

We stopped off at Brother Kevin's little hut on the way home. Brother Kevin was sitting on a log outside his front door covered from head to toe with wild birds. I suppose they'd got to know a soft touch when they saw one! He had coated himself with bread-crumbs and bits of bacon rind, and he was like a sort of running buffet for birds – except that he was sitting still, of course! I can't begin to describe the state of his robe, I'll have to leave it to your imagination. It might have started out brown, but it was rapidly turning whiter and whiter. Birds have no respect, none at all.

Maebh sat in the sun looking discontented. 'I'm bored!' she sighed. 'There's nothing to do here. And himself is no fun at all. Do you know he can't dance a single step, no not one? He can't jig or jump at all, and if he tries he either kicks himself or falls flat on his face, so he does.'

'I could learn!' a voice said from beneath a heap of birds. 'You could teach me! I'd try terrible hard to learn, just to please you, so I would.'

'But teaching someone to dance is *boring*. And I'm bored NOW!' she complained. 'So I'm not likely to be teaching you to dance any time soon, so don't be holding your breath at all, Kevin. And I'm fed up with these old clothes, and I don't like the food you cook, either. It's boring. I want strawberries and cream and candied plums.'

Ooh, I wanted to shake her!

'We just called in to say that you don't need to

worry about Conor of the Land Beneath,' Gwydion said, as reasonably as he could to a person he obviously wanted to bellow at. 'We managed to fool him with a fake version of you, and as long as the fake lasts, you aren't in any danger.'

'How could you possibly find anything that looks as lovely as me?' she asked. 'You must have used very powerful magic. How long will the pretend-me last?' she asked, sulkily.

'A week, I hope,' I said, crossing my fingers. 'But once it disappears, he's not going to be happy. He's going to be looking for me, I expect, and he'll certainly be looking for you. So you'd better take care if you go out and about. Keep your head down a bit. Basically, Maebh, stay here, inside, out of sight, all right?'

'Oh, but I'm not staying here!' she said, firmly. 'I'm coming with you, I am so.'

'Oh, no, you aren't!' I said, just as firmly. 'You aren't coming anywhere near Ynys Haf, ever again.'

'Well actually, Tanz,' Gwydion said uncomfortably, 'I've been thinking about that –'

Oh, no! He'd been thinking. That always meant trouble, right? Now what?

'– and I really think she should come back with us. That way we can keep an eye on her. Once Conor finds out that we've tricked him, he isn't going to be happy. Besides, anybody who helped us is going to be punished. Including Brother Kevin, if Conor discovers that he sheltered Maebh. And if Conor finds her actually here with him, heaven only knows what he might do.'

Brother Kevin's face emerged from behind a thrush's tail feathers. 'Ah, you've no call to worry yourselves about me, your honour. I'll be all right whatever Conor of the Land Beneath does. If he grabs me and takes me to his Land Beneath, sure and I might even try to change him into a decent sort of person. For a leprechaun, that is. Leprechauns are known to be entirely sneaky little creatures and could use some saving graces. Present company excepted,' he added hastily, remembering O'Liam and Siobhan.

'All the same,' Gwydion continued. 'I think Maebh should come back with us.'

I sighed. I recognised the expression on his face. It said: 'I'm Dragonking, and I insist. So there!'

So what could I do? We took Maebh with us. I suppose, actually, he was right. It would be dangerous to leave her there. We'd have to keep her well away from Master Henbane once we got back, though, or that might start up again. I thought we couldn't much trust Maebh, but I knew we couldn't trust Henbane!

It was a fairly uneventful journey after that: we managed to avoid Big Deirdre and the Bog Fairy and the Banshee. Gwydion and O'Liam found a boat and a boatman willing to take us across to Ynys Haf, and I was sea-sick the whole way.

When we landed at Gwyddno Garanhir's jetty we were all five of us whisked away to bed and tucked in with hot drinks and loving pats by Gwyddno's wife, and so it wasn't until the morning that we were able to meet King Gwyddno himself.

It was gone eleven when I woke. I found Gwydion tottering downstairs half-awake and unshaven.

'D'you think there'll be any breakfast left?' he asked hopefully. So we went and found the kitchen, and the friendly cook (who was remarkably thin for such a good cook) rustled us up some fresh mackerel fried in butter and oatmeal and fragrant, crusty bread fresh from the oven.

I was wiping the butter off my nose and burping contentedly when King Gwyddno appeared in the doorway. The cook curtseyed and made herself scarce, and Gwyddno came and sat at the wooden table with us. He grabbed a crust of bread, buttered it thickly and sloshed on some honey.

'Lady Garanhir said that there only the five of you?' he mumbled, his mouth full. 'Is that right? Not seven?'

I stared at him. 'No, not seven of us. Flissy and Nest are safely at home. Why were you expecting seven of us?'

Gwyddno put down his bread and butter and stared at me. Quite suddenly, I had a strange, sick feeling in the pit of my stomach. I looked at Gwydion and he stared back, worry chasing panic across his face, too.

'Well,' he said. 'Lady Haf, of course. T.A. She left here three days ago. Talked young Elffin into going with her, which was sensible, because T.A. knows nothing about Erin at all, and Elffin at least knows some of the hazards and pitfalls. He will take care of her. He's a good lad.'

And then I knew. I understood Conor of the Land Beneath's satisfied, crafty little smile. All the time we were there, somewhere in the Land Beneath he had T.A. under lock and key – or enchantment. And Elffin was with her. He had them both.

And we had tricked him with a false Maebh, and his revenge didn't bear thinking about when he discovered that he had let O'Liam go for nothing but a pile of straw and mud . . .

But now he had T.A.

What on earth was I going to do?

To be continued…